The *Curse* H a d Nine Lives

a novel by

Rich J. Stone

g l a r m
i n k
New York, New York

ISBN: 0981560911
EAN-13: 9780981560915
Published by Glarm Ink
Printed in the United States of America

For Raymond, Dashiell,
Dorothy and Agatha

ACKNOWLEDGMENTS

The author especially wishes to thank: Quiche Stone, Thomas Stone, Nahvae Frost, Greg Sanders, Larry Trivieri, Joan Black, Ann Kruse, Steven Solomon, Mom & Dad, Iago and Jeepster.

The Curse Had Nine Lives

Prolog.
Montgomery Maybach: A Family Curse

ACCORDING TO LEGEND, THE CURSE dated back to the Puritans and the Salem witch trials of 1692, where twenty innocent people were executed. In the mid-1700s, after the accused were posthumously exonerated, those families who led the witch hunt became pariahs. Forced to leave Salem, they fled north, and founded the quaint New England village of Olde Sayville, where centuries of curses proceeded to befall them. Suicides, poisonings, madness, strange "accidents"—the list of happenstances would become quite impressive, if only for the eeriness and unusually high mortality rate. And that was how it was for the Hawthornes of Olde Sayville. Until the Judge came along.

The Judge chose to reverse the curse. The first thing he did was remove the *"w"* from his name and changed it back to *Hathorne,* the way it was originally spelled when his unrepentant ancestor passed death sentences upon those accused of witchcraft in Salem. The family had tried to break with the past by altering the spelling of the name—the first to change it was Nathaniel Hawthorne, author of *The Scarlet Letter.* But to the Judge, *"w"* was the scarlet letter, and quite possibly the root cause of the curse—a shameful reminder of the denial of his Puritan heritage, which translated into an abandonment of Christian values; thus becoming an abomination in the eyes of God. It was when his second wife was stricken with cancer that the Judge attempted to recapture these Puritan values, and, in an act of proactive penance, founded the Olde Sayville Society, promoting temperance, devotion to the Almighty, and a newfound sense of community.

When I first came to Olde Sayville, there was little mention of the curse. Judge Hathorne was in his mid-seventies and celebrating his twentieth wedding anniversary to his third wife, Elizabeth. I was contracted to prepare the menu for the gala event. As it turned out, I made some life-long friends and returned every year thereafter to plan the banquet for the annual Olde Sayville Society Cat Show.

When the Judge died peacefully in his bed at the age of eighty-one, it seemed the curse was indeed reversed. Until the twenty-seventh day of May in the year 1996, that is. That was the day that Elizabeth Hathorne received the letter . . . and Bryce Danforth, the Olde Sayville Society's new director, decided to hire a private investigator from New York.

1.
Phil Dodge: A Cushy Gig

IT WAS A STRANGE PREOCCUPATION of the rich and powerful. Parading their pets around at their exclusive club, and awarding themselves prizes. And I couldn't understand why they needed a bodyguard. But the Olde Sayville Society was paying me more than I deserved, so who was I to say no? It was a welcome break from the slimeball jobs I normally booked. My last couple of gigs were real ball-breakers. I was hired to obtain photographic evidence of some sap's wife banging his best friend—I showed him the pictures at which point he promptly cancelled his insurance policy and blew his brains out. Problem was he neglected to pay me before he did himself in. For my next job, I was looking for a missing person, who wasn't missing so much as hiding from the abusive shit that hired me to find her. I located her for him. She had taken to turning tricks to make ends meet, and when that same abusive shit tried to yank her from her street corner, her pimp put three bullets through him for "poaching on one of his bitches." So a working vacation in New England was just what the doctor ordered—literally. I had been warned that if I didn't take it easy, my bleeding ulcer would put me in the hospital. And after my last couple of cases, it felt as if I had a tiny gymnast competing for the gold in my stomach. So my doctor put in a good word for me to his old college chum, Bryce Danforth, one of the Olde Sayville Society officers. "After a week or so in

Olde Sayville, you'll feel better than you have in twenty-five years," my doctor told me. My twenty-five-year anniversary of being a private investigator was fast approaching—it didn't take a genius to connect the dots.

I looked out the window—nothing but lush views of charming New England scenery—and it bored the living hell out of me. As the train chugged along through the rustic wilderness, I re-read the so-called poisoned pen letter:

> *Make sure you JUDGE properly at the CAT show.*
> *It will become APPARENT to you who should*
> *win. It should also be apparent what will happen*
> *to you if you fail to make the PROPER decision.*
> *REMEMBER: There is a CURSE on your family.*

A family curse? I laughed out loud, attracting odd stares from the other passengers. I smiled at an attractive woman seated across the aisle from me, a few rows up. She blushed and quickly stuck her head back into her book. Then she nonchalantly tugged her skirt up an inch or six to reveal a bit more of her legs. Naturally, I went over to introduce myself. As I got closer, I saw that she was reading *The Great Gatsby*. As luck would have it, it was one of the few books that I'd actually read. Back in high school, I never did any of the assigned readings; I spent all my spare time in the schoolyard. But *Gatsby* happened to be the book that was assigned right after I broke my collar bone when a fight broke out during a game of "no rules" broom hockey, so while I was laid up at home with nothing better to do, I gave it a read.

"Great book," I said, as I slid myself down into the seat next to her.

"Is that why you came over here? You wanna start a book club?" she asked playfully.

As I tried to produce a witty comeback/come-on, the conductor called out my stop.

"You wouldn't by any chance be getting off in Olde Sayville?" I asked her.

"I'm afraid not," she said, twirled her hair, batted her eyelashes, shrugged her shoulders and, having run out of flirtatious maneuvers, returned her attention to Gatsby.

"Pity," I said, rising from my seat. "Sure I can't persuade you to change your plans? How 'bout I buy you a drink and you catch a later train?"

She looked up at me and smiled. "Let me guess," she said. "First time in Olde Sayville?"

"Yeah," I said, smiling back. "How did you know?"

"You'll find out soon enough." Then she blew me a kiss and waved goodbye. "Perhaps we're destined to meet again," she said.

"If the planets line up just right," I answered, and made my way to the exit.

When I got off the train, I was greeted by one of the Olde Sayville aristocracy. A fat guy wearing plaid knickers extended his stubby-fingered hand.

"Mr. Dodge, I presume?" he asked proudly, seemingly amused with his powers of deduction. I was the only person to get off the train without a sweater draped around his neck. A dead giveaway.

"That's right," I said. I took the chubby, limp hand and formulated a poor excuse for a handshake.

"Montgomery Maybach," he said, introducing himself. "Very pleased to make your acquaintance."

I looked off toward the road. A dark blue Rolls Royce was parked at the curb, complemented by a dapper middle-aged chauffeur, dressed to the hilt, standing at its side. The stubby fingers waved to the chauffeur, who presented himself immediately. It was a like a scene out of *Gatsby*, except I wasn't a gate-crasher—I was actually invited.

"This is Rudolf," the knickers-wearing Maybach said. "He'll

attend to your luggage." He looked around for a moment. "Where *is* your luggage?"

"You guys told me not to bring any, remember? Said you'd have me outfitted to blend in with the crowd." Actually, it didn't matter whether they had told me that or not. I'm notorious for being a light packer. My rule of thumb: If it doesn't fit in my coat, I don't bring it.

"But ... perhaps some toiletries, or a good book, maybe . . . ?" he asked.

I let his words dangle there. In the uncomfortable silence that followed, Maybach shrugged and extended his fat arm in the direction of the Rolls. Rudolf opened the door for me and I got in. There was an interesting odor in there that I couldn't make out—I figured it was just the smell of old money. As I stretched my legs out in front of me, surveying the more than ample leg room, Maybach leaned his bloated, multi-chinned face into the window.

"I must retrieve some precious goods from the groomers," he offered unsolicited. "My cats Dashiell and Lillian are showing this week. Rudolf will drive you to the club and get you acquainted."

Maybach spun around and wobbled toward a Mercedes convertible that was parked a few yards away. I leaned back and got comfortable in the Rolls as Rudolf gently pulled the car out of the station road. Within minutes we were traveling on an old country drive flanked by weeping willow trees. There wasn't another car around us for miles. I pinched myself to make sure I wasn't dreaming. What a cushy gig this was—play bodyguard for some rich widow, and make sure no cheating went on in a cat show. What a laugh. I didn't know what was more ridiculous: me as a cat show rules enforcer, or the fact these people took it so seriously. But I could understand the fanaticism, I suppose. Back in 1994, I made a deal with God that if He let the Rangers win the Stanley Cup, thereby ending their fifty-four-year curse, I'd never complain about anything else, ever again. God kept his side, and gave them a Stanley Cup title on June 14, 1994. I didn't keep mine, though, and in August of 1994, I complained to God again. I welshed on the Almighty. And He didn't like it. Within a week, the baseball players went on strike and the World Series was cancelled that year. Then the hockey players had a labor dispute, and when they finally agreed to play a shortened season, the Rangers' hated cross-Hudson rivals ended up winning the Cup. Suffice it to say, God and I were no longer on speaking terms. So maybe I was destined to be here—almost two years to the day that the Rangers won the Cup—as a bodyguard at the Olde Sayville Society cat show. The very thought gave me a craving for a shot of whiskey. I asked Rudolf if there was a place to get a quick drink.

"I'm supposed to take you directly to the club. There's plenty of soda and lemonade there."

"Although that sounds just lovely, Rudolf, I'd prefer something more along the lines of a bar."

"There are no bars, Mr. Dodge," Rudolf answered. "Olde Sayville is a dry town."

He is a vengeful God, indeed.

2.

Maybach: A Tale of Two Kitties

I HURRIED INTO THE GROOMING SALON and greeted my feline darlings. Normally I'd remain with my Persian beauties through the entire grooming process, but today I had to tend to the unpleasant business of meeting and greeting Philip Dodge at the train depot. The Society could dress him up all they liked, but no Ralph Lauren creation could mask that gruffness. He didn't seem the right fit at all to take on the job. I doubted that he would take the curse seriously.

I was against the whole idea of bringing in an outside investigator, but Bryce wouldn't have it any other way. Once Elizabeth Hathorne received the letter, she was shaken and refused to judge without a protector. The letter was not something to be taken lightly, certainly—I'd already seen my share of poisoned pen letters lead to murder. Each of them solved by yours truly, ably assisted by Dash and Lil, of course. I suppose that's what was really gnawing at me. Why did Bryce feel the need to bring in Dodge when he had me?

"He's not so much an investigator as a bodyguard," Bryce told me; but even through his broad trademark smile, his words seemed empty to me—just a thinly veiled attempt to spare my feelings. Granted, Dodge was in much better shape than I. My three-hundred-pound carriage wasn't particularly suited to hand-to-hand combat. Perhaps this was a matter for a more—shall we say—agile presence. And, at first glance, Dodge's physical attributes appeared to fit the bill nicely—over six-feet tall, and in seemingly good shape—however, on closer inspection he displayed a rather weathered and weary demeanor. He may not have brought any luggage with him, but the bags under his eyes looked like they could carry a double-valise's worth. It left me with the distinct impression that his best years were well behind him. Certainly a much more refined presence was required. I'm sure in the big city there's a need for brawn, but doubtless our letter writer would be too clever to be deterred by this bull-in-a-china-shop approach. I popped a truffle into my mouth to relieve the tension. I didn't want to appear ill-at-ease in front of Dash and Lil. This was the first year that I'd been invited to enter my own cats in the show—the first time in the history of the Olde Sayville Society Cat Show that an "outsider" was permitted. While I was extremely honored, I was also a bit apprehensive. The cat show had enormous significance to the residents of Olde Sayville; some even believed that it had a connection to the curse itself. To me, however, it was just another way to show off how special my Dashiell and Lillian were. But now that there was talk of the curse resurfacing, I feared that my inclusion in the show would be blamed for it. Although I counted the Olde Sayville Society members among my friends, I knew there was a line that couldn't be crossed—not being a descendant of Salem, there would always be some sort of social chasm between me and the members. So much so, I shudder to think what they would say if they knew that my family didn't cross the Atlantic until the 1820s.

Dash squinted at me when I entered the room, then aloofly averted his gaze. Lil was a little more forgiving and let me scratch her behind the ears. It was Lil's need for attention that had alerted me to the real killer in a case some years back. A man had murdered his wife—she had threatened to leave him and expose him as a foot fetishist in open court unless he agreed to a very large alimony settlement. He killed her and made it look like a suicide. Lil was striving for my attention and knocked a piece of bric-a-brac from a curio into a trash can where we discovered shredded documents. After painstakingly piecing them together, I discovered they comprised an earlier draft of the suicide note, and several photos of feet in compromising positions. Not an easy case to forget.

I released the precious felines from their carrier as soon as I reached my hotel room, wondering if Dash and Lil would be of any assistance to Elizabeth Hathorne. How could I entrust Elizabeth's well-being to the thuggish has-been that I had met at the train station? I decided to drop in on Bryce at the Society before Dodge had the opportunity to muck things up and endanger Elizabeth's life even more.

3.
Dodge: A "Dry" Sense of Humor

A MOUTH JAMMED FULL OF BRIGHT WHITE PERFECT TEETH jabbered away while I sipped my virginal lemonade.

"So, as you see," the mouth continued through a plastered on grin, "we have quite a situation here."

"And you only need me to make sure nothing happens to the widow, right?" I asked. "You don't want me to try and find out who's responsible?"

Bryce Danforth licked his lips and flashed me a perfect smile. I had to momentarily avert my gaze—the combination of his white teeth and shiny silver hair was practically blinding. "The police have assured me that they have the best men working on it."

"That's good enough for me," I said. "Standing aside and letting the cops do their job is usually the best for everybody." I was lying, of course. Twenty-five years on the job had taught me to take nothing for granted and to trust no one.

"Then I'm glad we understand each other," Danforth said. "It's what the Old Judge would have wanted." He gestured to an enormous portrait of a very sober-looking, robed gentleman hanging on the wall behind his desk. The angle of the sunlight pouring through the window gave the Judge a golden halo. I noticed a marble bust on the desk that sported the same profile. What did the Bible say about idol worship?

"Was that his?" I asked, pointing to an empty wheelchair in the corner near the window.

"Yes," Bryce answered. "In his later years he had some trouble getting around. We haven't found a place to put it yet."

"That's the problem with these sprawling estates," I said. "Never enough closets."

Bryce laughed by emitting a few snorts, making the alligator logo on his shirt look like it was having an epileptic seizure.

"So when do I get to meet the Judge's old lady?" I asked.

"Oh, she's not at all old," he quickly responded. "I'll introduce you to her shortly."

I absentmindedly took a sip of lemonade. Bryce focused on the disappointed look on my face.

"How's your lemonade? Not too sour?"

"Not at all. In fact, it could use a little bite."

The teeth formed a slightly less angelic grin. "You are aware that this is a dry town, Mr. Dodge," he said loudly, presumably for the benefit of anyone who might happen to be listening at the door. He walked to the window and lowered the Venetian blinds. It cast shadows on the Judge's portrait, removing the halo and replacing it with prison bars. But it looked like we were in the cell and the Judge was looking down on us through the bars, ready to pass sentence. And when Danforth drew the blinds shut, all the vibrant color washed out of the portrait as it seemingly turned to shades of gray. Danforth gave me a sly wink as he approached the colorless, ominous-looking Judge mounted on the wall behind the desk. He pushed the portrait aside to reveal a wall safe. Aha, I thought. The perfect scarecrow.

Bryce reached inside the safe, past stacks of money and assorted papers, and pulled out an ornate glass-and-metal decanter. My lemonade was about to be substantially improved. That is, until there was a limp tapping at the door. Bryce Danforth quickly returned the contraband to the safe and locked away my hopes of a quick fix behind the scowling, and no doubt, disapproving Old Judge. He opened the door and Montgomery Maybach waddled in.

"Monty," exclaimed Danforth. "Just the fellow I wanted to see. Have you met Mr. Dodge?"

"Briefly, yes," Maybach moped. "Have you filled in Mr. Dodge on the details of the Hathorne case, Bryce?"

"The details of the Hathorne case?" I repeated.

"Monty is a bit of an amateur sleuth," Danforth added.

"Great!" I said, dripping with sarcasm. I couldn't believe I was being denied alcohol because this pompous chubb-o needed to prance around playing detective.

"I'll have you know, I've solved six cases in the last two years alone," he said. "Quite frankly, sometimes I don't even know why they bother to pay the police."

It was time to put fatty in his place. "What exactly are the qualifications for *amateur* sleuthing?" I asked, baiting him. "I mean, aside from having no training, no license, and no one ever actually hiring you?"

Maybach stared at me, but didn't lose his temper. Didn't even seem offended. Seemed more proud than hurt. "It's more of a calling, actually," he said. "And I'll wager that I find the author of these letters before you do."

"Well, you may have an advantage," I said. "You may be the one who wrote them."

Without missing a beat, Maybach shrugged off my loaded statement and shot back: "Yes, that would be quite an advantage, wouldn't it?" He wasn't as much of a foppish ego case as I'd thought. Perhaps he could be helpful in providing some background for me. Especially since Bryce Danforth wasn't giving me a helluva lot of information and was perfectly content to let the cops handle it.

"So what's your take on the letter, Maybach?" I asked.

"A club member, I'd imagine. It would have to be someone who knows about the curse, since it hasn't really been a subject of conversation for years."

"Not to be rude," I said, "but, no shit, Agatha."

Maybach bristled slightly and then took it in stride.

"Perhaps I should take you around and introduce you to the club members," he said.

"Not until I'm undercover," I said.

"Yes, good point," Bryce added. "Monty, why don't you take him over to Elizabeth's house first and introduce them? Then, after he's been properly attired, we'll have Mr. Dodge assimilate with the members."

Assimilate. Interesting word choice, but probably accurate. He was about to introduce a stray, mangy mutt into his perfectly groomed, pure-bred society.

"Maybach can fill me in on each of the suspects before I meet them," I said. "That'll put me at an advantage."

"I'll call Elizabeth and let her know you're on your way," Bryce said, politely shooing us out of the office.

"What about my retainer?" I said to Bryce. "I don't exactly have piles of cash lying around like most of the citizens here. If my wallet is a bit thicker, it'll make the assimilation process that much easier."

Bryce blushed, flashed me that winning grin, dug into his pocket and pulled two fresh C-notes off a money clip that would need a team of accountants to figure out they were missing. "Will a couple of hundred do you for now?"

"Thanks," I said pocketing the cash. "Now I'll be able to buy that yacht I've always wanted. Unless I end up blowing it on something extravagant, like rent or food."

Predictably, Bryce grinned, then continued to gently guide us out of his office. I gave Maybach a quick nod, and we retreated to his Mercedes. Maybach was a fairly able driver despite the fact that his arms were so thick he had trouble bending them. It looked like two giant hams attached to a steering wheel. Out on the open road I asked Maybach where he was hiding it.

"Hiding what?" he asked.

"The hooch. I know you've got some. You gourmet types wouldn't be caught dead without a few bottles for mealtime."

"I have three bottles of wine back at the hotel. That is the legal limit that can be brought into this town and I intend to drink them myself. Besides, we haven't the time for that now. Elizabeth Hathorne is expecting us."

"Assuming that Bryce called her," I said.

"He did. Bryce is very reliable that way."

"But not so much in other ways?" I asked.

"What are you suggesting?" Maybach asked.

"He's a tad full of shit, isn't he?" I shot back.

"Well, of course he is," he said matter-of-factly. "Bryce Danforth is one of the most disingenuous humans on God's green earth. You don't need to be a licensed private investigator to figure that one out."

"Touché, Maybach. Touché."

Maybach proceeded to fill me in on the other club members with agonizingly dull detail. There was Bryce's nephew, Samuel "Chip" Danforth, the club's golf champ until last year when he double-bogeyed on the eighteenth hole allowing Eliot "Biff" Stoughton to claim the title, even though Eliot has a nervous condition which sometimes affects his putting. And Eliot's first cousin, Blake, was recently initiated, but he has a food allergy, so the banquet menu had to be redone at the last minute. And on and on and on. For the next eight or nine members that Maybach mentioned, he concentrated more on their eating habits than anything else. And, of course—according to Monty, at least—they were all above reproach and couldn't be considered as suspects. My mind went numb. There used to be a time when I was actually selective about which cases I'd take. Now my only two criteria were "how much?" and "when can you pay me?" This case had already passed both tests with flying colors.

✳ ✳ ✳

ELIZABETH HATHORNE LIVED IN A MANSION ON A HILL. It was a winding, tree-lined road that ascended to a four-car garage. From there, a cobblestone walkway led to the main house. It was slightly amusing watching Maybach struggle with the uneven path, but hearing his deep wheezes as we walked up the few steps to the porch made me feel a little sorry for him. He was sweating profusely by the time we made it to the doorbell. I rang it, so Maybach wouldn't need to exert any more energy, while at the same time, sparing myself from being exposed to the ever-growing sweat stain that had formed under Maybach's arm. A gray, slightly hunched woman answered the door.

"Hello, Wanda dear," Maybach said between gasps for breath. "We're here to see Mrs. Hathorne."

"Yes," she said. "Mr. Danforth telephoned. We've been expecting you."

We entered the mansion, and Wanda led us to a sitting room with an enormous bay window. The walls were covered with portraits—all of them prominently featuring the Judge.

"Wait here, please," she said and galumphed out of the room. Maybach perched himself on a divan, which buckled in the middle when he sat down. I examined the art work.

"Is that Mrs. Hathorne?" I asked Maybach, pointing to a portrait of the Judge with a cowering woman at his side. Fear seemed to be etched across her face.

"The first Mrs. Hathorne, yes. She died almost forty years ago."

"Are you sure she wasn't just using that as an excuse?" I wisecracked, doing a poor Groucho Marx impersonation. "What about this one?" I asked pointing to a different submissive woman in another portrait.

"That was the second Mrs. Hathorne. She died about a year after the first Mrs. Hathorne."

"Any likenesses of the current Mrs. Hathorne in here?"

"No," Maybach answered dryly, "just the dead ones."

I heard footsteps approaching, so I decided to keep my art observations to myself. A set of legs entered the room and introduced themselves.

"I'm Elizabeth Hathorne. You must be Mr. Dodge."

I looked upward and saw a sleek, firm body, and elegantly pretty face attached to the legs. With ever-so-slightly-graying long, brown hair pulled back tight against her head, Elizabeth Hathorne was a radiant beauty. I took her extended hand and went one step further, by cradling her sleeveless arm and pressing her soft hand to my lips. I figured I could get away with that sort of thing in this society—it might read as chivalrous. I lingered for a moment. She smelled good.

"At your service," I said. "A pleasure to meet you, Mrs. Hathorne."

"Please, call me Elizabeth."

She had a sweet, calm and angelic voice. How could the Judge have possibly looked so angry in all those pictures?

"Then you must call me Phil," I said, unconsciously shifting into full flirtation mode; it seems that whenever I'm around an incredibly beautiful woman, I go into autopilot. I arched an eyebrow and gazed into her blue-green eyes. For some strange reason, I was immediately filled with warmth—a warmth that I hadn't felt since . . . well . . . ever. But the moment was all too fleeting.

"And, of course, you may continue to call me Monty," Maybach spoke up from the bowed divan.

"Monty," Elizabeth exclaimed. "I'm so sorry; I didn't even see you there."

While Maybach struggled to raise himself from the divan, Elizabeth walked past the bay window and bent over to greet him, showing off her incredibly perfect ass. But my attention was quickly diverted. At that precise moment, the window shattered, the divan crumpled and Monty fell flat on his far-from-perfect ass. Apparently, someone had fired a bullet through the window, which narrowly missed Elizabeth and embedded itself squarely in one of the divan's already heavily taxed legs, causing its collapse.

I hit the deck and crawled through some broken glass toward the window. I slowly lifted my head above the sill and looked for any signs of the perp. It looked like a quick shoot and run, with only one shot fired. Possibly more of a scare tactic than a murder attempt, but the bullet landed too close to the target to be sure.

"Call the police," I ordered the widow. "Tell them exactly what happened." Right after she left the room, I used every bit of my strength to pull Maybach to his feet.

"I need you to give me a quick tour of the terrain," I said. "I need to see it all before the cops get here and close it off."

The tiny gymnast in my stomach did a ten-point dismount onto my spleen. My restful retreat had lasted less than two hours.

4.
Maybach: A Walk in the Woods

DODGE WAS TRYING TO KILL ME. He didn't care that my heart was about to explode. He just kept pushing me deeper and deeper into the wooded hills surrounding the Hathorne estate. He moved swiftly, examining the ground. He carried a small camera with him and snapped photos of the dirt, the trees, and the landscape. My heart was already pounding from the murder attempt. Had the bullet been a bit higher, it would have lodged right between my eyes.

Finally, after Dodge had seen and photographed all there was to see and photograph, we returned to the mansion and awaited the arrival of the dimwitted Olde Sayville police force. We made a detour and stopped at the car first. I craved some brandy to calm my nerves. Whenever I visited Olde Sayville, I packed a box of liqueur-filled chocolates for the trip. It was my little secret liquor cabinet. I suppose that qualified me as an unadulterated Chocoholic. After plunging a few of them into my mouth, I thought about my dear friend, Geoffrey, an accomplished food critic. Not only did he give me my first big break in the food industry by writing a wonderful review about my catering business, it was Geoffrey who strategized the plan to conceal my illegal alcoholic pleasures inside chocolate—"a more dignified version of the hash brownie," as he called it.

I took enough magical chocolates with me to keep my mouth

occupied during the hike from my car back to the mansion. By the time we reached the sitting room, the soothing effects of the chocolates had begun to sink in, and I was able to concentrate once again on the recent events. Who could have fired that shot? I went through a list of possible suspects in my head. Right now that was everybody, except Elizabeth, Dodge and myself. I turned to Dodge.

"I'll get you a list of everyone who is entered in the cat show," I said. "Then we can parse it down to probable and improbable suspects, yes?"

Dodge looked down at me with his dark brown eyes shooting daggers. Then he rubbed his stomach, turned his head and stared off toward the woods through the shattered grand bay window. He seemed perturbed by my suggestion.

"I'm sorry if I insulted you, Mr. Dodge, but I believe it's in everyone's best interests if we work on this case together."

Dodge turned his icy stare back in my direction and ripped in. "Okay, Maybach. Go compile a list. When you're done you can leave it for me in that garbage can over there."

Dodge was intimidating, to be sure; but I was never one to back down.

"Why do you refuse my help?" I countered. "Certainly the cat show contestants rank up there as suspects."

"Do you actually think anyone gives a shit about the fucking cat show?" Dodge said in a loud whisper, trying to control his rage. It was the second time I'd heard profanity generate from between his thin lips. Alas, it wouldn't be the last time, either.

"As a matter of fact, I firmly believe that people *do* care about the cat show," I asserted. "It's a matter of great pride here. You have absolutely no idea."

"Give me a break. A cat show?" he said with annoyance.

"Not a cat person, are you, Mr. Dodge?"

"No."

"Although, you don't exactly strike me as a dog person

either," I said.

"No, Monty," Dodge snapped back. "I'm a fucking people person."

Luckily the doorbell rang. The police had finally arrived—it took them nearly thirty minutes to answer a call for attempted murder in a town no larger than twenty square miles. Pathetic. Dodge rubbed his stomach and exited the sitting room to greet the police. It was apparent that Dodge wanted no part in a co-investigation. His reluctance, coupled with the local police force's total incompetence, meant that it was up to Dashiell, Lillian and me to reveal the letter writer and attempted murderer. Elizabeth Hathorne's life depended on it.

ﮬ ﮬ ﮬ

AFTER THE POLICE QUESTIONED DODGE, Wanda escorted him upstairs to his room, and presumably introduced him to his new wardrobe. It was now my turn to be interviewed by the police. The officer in charge looked like he was twelve years old and I fully expected his voice to change during the course of the questioning. I answered each of the questions posed to me, and then excused myself. I needed to get back to my hotel and check on Dash and Lil, then to the club to fill Bryce in on the day's activities. Dodge would be able to look after Elizabeth. The way he looked at her, I had no trouble believing that he would take a bullet for her if necessary.

I bade farewell to Elizabeth just before the police began to question her, and headed toward the cobbled path. Another quick chocolate for the road seemed in order. Except that my Mercedes was nowhere to be found. And when I burst back into the house, Phil Dodge was nowhere to be found either.

5.
Dodge: A Joy Ride

THE FOLKS AT MERCEDES made a very nice automobile. No doubt about it. And I felt very much at home. I didn't even have to adjust the seat; my long legs seemed to counter-balance Maybach's midsection. I was now dressed in tennis whites, with a fancy v-neck sweater topping off the preppy uniform for good measure. I felt like an F. Scott Fitzgerald character, except without the booze.

The police interview was a joke. It was easy to turn the tables on them and I ended up asking them more questions than they asked me. Thus far, their so-called investigation of the letter had turned up squat and they weren't taking the threat too seriously. Translation: they were afraid to put pressure on any of the influential club members. I knew a lot of big city cops who were corrupt, but that was usually out of greed, not out of fear. The Olde Sayville cops were more like a police force of puppets—clearly out of their league.

I was ready to start interviewing club members and I didn't want Maybach anywhere near me when I did. Maybach was too close to the Olde Sayville Society culture not to be influenced one way or another. So stealing his car seemed to be the only viable solution. I pulled into the Olde Sayville Society parking lot and prepared my undercover persona. Tennis anyone? I felt like a dork. A big, rich, sober dork. I decided to drop in on Bryce Danforth first, in hopes of getting a quick whiskey fix.

My prayers were answered. When I barged into Bryce's

office unannounced, I discovered Bryce sitting in the Judge's old wheelchair, having himself a little drink; the Venetian blinds, of course, were still drawn shut.

"No wonder you haven't found a place for that yet. It's your special drinking chair, isn't it?" I asked.

"Thank God it's only you," he said, relieved that I wasn't some temperance-minded club member. "Nice outfit, by the way," Bryce added, flashing me his bright white teeth. He rose from the wheelchair and poured himself another round from the decanter. "Grab a glass," he said. I complied and drank a tumbler of the smoothest Scotch I'd ever tasted.

"Why are you here, Bryce?" I asked.

"This is my office."

"No," I clarified, "why are you in this town? At this club? You obviously don't share the values. Why not relocate?"

"My wife," he answered.

"What about her?"

"She's . . . she's very happy here." Then he just stared into his glass for a minute or so. After a painfully uncomfortable silence, he emptied his glass, and returned the decanter to the wall safe. He walked to the window, opened the Venetian blinds—now that the contraband was safely cached—and stared out the window. He seemed to be looking at a couple on the tennis courts. An attractive woman with large breasts served the ball to her partner, an agile blond man, who hit the ball back right to her. Sadly, she didn't even have to move to return it, cheating me of the thrill of watching her boobs jiggling about. The rally went on for several shots. The blond man ran all over the court, but—dammit—always hit the ball right back to the woman's forehand. Finally the woman hit the ball into the net. Then she giggled and playfully wagged her finger at the man.

"Who are they?" I asked.

"That would be my wife, Lydia," he said, "with our resident tennis pro, Lloyd Proctor."

I tried to come up with something to say, but came up empty. What could I say? Comment on his wife's forehand? Tell him she had a great set of knockers? Ask him if he thought she was fucking the strapping blond guy? Finally, Bryce turned around and motioned toward the door.

"So, are you ready to meet the members?" he asked, much more upbeat, trying to put a happy face on his empty existence. He pulled two breath mints from his pocket and offered me one of them. We needed to conceal our crime.

"Let's go," I said, taking the mint and popping it into my mouth. "By the way, did you notice any members arriving or departing in the last hour or so?"

Bryce shrugged. "I wouldn't know. I've been busy." He winked, and tossed the other breath mint into his mouth. Even though I'd known Bryce Danforth less than three hours, I was already his confidant. His secret drinking buddy. I'd seen his kind before. I realized that if I could get a few more drinks in him, he'd reveal every ugly detail about every club member. And in the name of protecting Elizabeth Hathorne, it was exactly what I intended to do.

We stepped out into the main room of the Society clubhouse, a large ballroom, which could only be considered modest when comparing it to the Vatican. The first person Bryce introduced me to was his twenty-five-year-old nephew, Chip Danforth, a tall, good-looking kid with a pleasant demeanor. Maybe it was just my gut instinct, but I had come to distrust people with pleasant demeanors. "Do people call you Chip because you have a good golf game?" I asked him. I recalled Maybach had said something about Chip Danforth choking on the final hole in the club's annual golf tournament, so maybe it was still a sore spot and I could elicit some raw emotional response from the kid. But I was wrong. He was as even-tempered and polished as they come.

"Oh no, Mr. Dodge," he said. "I've been called Chip ever since I was a little boy—long before I ever picked up my first golf club." He grinned and showed off his perfect white smile. Apparently it was a Danforth family trait.

"Will you be showing at the cat show?" I asked.

"Yes, sir. Cleopatra and I wouldn't miss it for the world."

"I'll keep an eye out for her," I said.

"She'll be easy to spot. She's the only Sphinx entered."

Bryce had broken away from the conversation and was motioning me to come over to meet another member, who looked like he might die before I made it across the room to him. Chip and I exchanged handshakes.

"By the way," I said before turning to go, "was that you I just saw pulling into the parking lot? Driving a . . . oh, what do you call those things?"

"It's a Lamborghini. Yes, that was me."

My bluff worked.

"Beautiful car. Fast?"

"Very. Eliot Stoughton has one, too. But mine's definitely faster."

So that was everything I needed to know about Chip Danforth: twenty-five years old, has a show cat named Cleopatra, owns a Lamborghini that he likes to drive fast, and never had to work a day in his life. No wonder he was smiling.

"Well, nice meeting you, Chip," I said, trying not to let my jealousy show. I walked over to Bryce, who was in deep conversation with a severely elderly gent, whose scowl wasn't radically different from that of the Judge in all the portraits. He had a slight resemblance to Mark Twain, with a thick white head of hair and bushy white eyebrows. Rudolf, the Olde Sayville Society's chauffeur, stood behind him, at the ready to catch the old man in case he lost his balance.

"I'd like you to meet the Colonel," Bryce said.

The Colonel was the only surviving charter member. And in deference to this status, Bryce took it upon himself to blow my cover.

"Mr. Dodge is an investigator from New York. He'll be protecting Elizabeth Hathorne."

"I expect you'll do a fine job," the Colonel said to me. "Otherwise you'll be held accountable."

Accountable? I let the statement go unchallenged for the moment. As my cover was blown, there was nothing to be gained.

"Well, let's just keep it to ourselves, then, that I'm a private investigator. The best way for me to protect her is for no one to know what I'm doing."

"Loose lips sink ships," the Colonel blurted out. Then abruptly, he turned and walked away. Rudolf sighed, shrugged his shoulders and dutifully followed behind the Colonel. I looked at Bryce, who was all teeth.

"Why is he called the Colonel? Was he in the military?"

"No," Bryce said. "He's a doctor actually. 'Colonel' is a nickname the Judge gave him fifty years ago. No one really knows why."

"Does he?"

"I'm sure at one time he did. These days . . . I'm not so certain. Ever since his wife passed away he's been getting stranger and stranger. Poor Rudolf—he's taken it upon himself to look out for the old man, but I think he bit off more than he can chew."

Bryce laughed. I laughed, too. Not because I thought the Colonel's eroding mental capability was funny, but just to be polite. Perhaps my goofy apparel was rubbing off on me. Bryce then directed my attention to a pair of men a few yards away, who looked like a young preppy version of Abbott and Costello.

"That's Eliot Stoughton," he said, referring to the taller one, "with his cousin, Blake Giles."

"Eliot's the new golf champ, yes?"

"Yes," Bryce said. "How did you know?"

"I'm a private investigator. It's my business to know."

"Tell me something else about him," Bryce challenged.

"He has a nervous condition, he drives a Lamborghini, and his nickname is Biff," I said. Bryce seemed impressed. We walked over and Bryce introduced me to Stoughton and Giles.

Eliot Stoughton blinked a lot. And twitched. And stammered occasionally. His line of vision was aimed straight at the floor, refusing to make eye contact. He was obviously ill-at-ease with strangers. His ability to make a good first impression was totally absent—a complete social retard. The kind of person who would never be called back for a second job interview. Of course, he didn't have to worry about a job, since he had inherited obscene amounts of money and land from his daddy, who, in turn, inherited it from his daddy, and so on and so on and so on.

"I hear you're the club's golf champ," I said to him, trying to ease him out of his awkward state. But that only made him twitch more, causing his gangly arms to flail slightly.

"He sure is," Blake Giles said, answering for his socially inept cousin. "Kicked Chip's butt on the back nine." Blake was a short, stocky, cocky kid. An air of arrogance emanated from him.

"Blake!" Eliot shrieked. His eyes had taken a rest from staring at the floor and began a series of rapid blinking, leading to a display of facial ticks. "Sh-sh-show a little decorum." Stoughton turned to me, making semi-eye contact for the first time. "My apologies, Mr. Dodge. Blake is still quite young."

"Just proud of his cousin, I suppose," I said. I looked straight into Eliot's blinking eyes and refused to break the stare. I could sense Eliot's unease.

"So, w-what brings you to Olde Sayville, Mr. Dodge?" he asked.

"The cat show, of course," I answered. I held my gaze on Eliot for another five seconds or so, then mercifully broke it off and turned toward Blake. "Planning on kicking Cleopatra's ass, too?"

Blake produced a short staccato laugh that sounded like a

high-pitched machine gun. "That's a foregone conclusion. A Sphinx has a snowball's chance in hell of winning." Cocky kid. I'd met his type before; he was someone who desperately needed to have his ass kicked. Normally, I'd be more than happy to oblige, but at the moment, I was still undercover.

Just then I heard a loud huff, quickly followed by a long wheeze, and punctuated by a loud puff. I didn't need to look in the direction of the sounds. It was fairly clear that Montgomery Maybach had arrived. I met him halfway, fearing his heart would stop if he had to traverse the entire ballroom floor.

"Car thief!" he said through a gasp for air. "How could you? Of all the lowdown skullduggery I would have expected of you, you've gone and surpassed that."

"How's the widow?" I asked.

"A little shaken, but much better than I expected. She was kind enough to drive me here after the police were done questioning her."

"I would have thought she'd have a chauffeur to drive her around," I said.

"Today's his day off. And Wanda's far too aged to drive." While I made a mental note to question the chauffeur, Maybach turned his attention to Bryce, who had just made his way over to us. "Unbelievable, Bryce, isn't it?"

"What is?" Bryce asked.

"He's just sore because I borrowed his car without asking," I said. Bryce snorted out a chuckle and flashed a big Danforth grin.

"I was referring to the murder attempt," Maybach said.

Bryce's smile disappeared. "Oh my God. Is Elizabeth all right?"

"She's fine," I said before Maybach had a chance to answer. "The attempt was on Monty, here." I stared at Maybach, hoping he would get my drift and play along.

"Yes. I thought so, too," he said without missing a beat. "I swear, Bryce, a foot or two higher, and I'd be dead."

Bryce looked puzzled. I related the story to him, except I made it appear that Maybach was the intended victim. Then I launched into the "theory" segment.

"I think the poisoned pen author is seeking to eliminate the competition. Your cats are pretty formidable, aren't they, Monty?"

"Um, well, yes," he responded. "Yes, they are."

"And very capable of being top dog at the cat show, right?"

"Yes," he said, "although you may wish to use a different metaphor in the future."

Bryce just nodded his silvery head up and down, while staring off into space. "This is very troubling," he finally said, then turned to me. "Why didn't you tell me this before?"

"I didn't want to kill your mood, if you know what I mean. I was planning on telling you after the introductions were done with. Didn't want to cast a pall over it." I lied again. Lying was my standard M.O.—borne out of my total distrust of everyone.

"I can appreciate that," Bryce said. Then he excused himself and set out for his office. No doubt he would be consulting with the stash behind the Judge.

"Let's go," I said to Maybach, and handed him his car keys. "We've got a lot to talk about."

6.
Maybach: A Difference of Opinion

TYPICALLY, PHIL DODGE WAS A MAN OF FEW WORDS. He was keen on observation and left the talking to others. But on the ten-minute drive back to my hotel he spoke the entire time. And there was much profanity. To summarize (and sanitize), he told me to stay away from the investigation, that I was just mucking (although he didn't exactly use the word "mucking") things up, and if he needed me for anything, he would ask. Then he asked me to drive him to Elizabeth Hathorne's house. I drove to my hotel instead. I needed to check on Dash and Lil.

"I'm warning you, Maybach," Dodge said to me as we entered my room, "anything happens to the widow tonight, it's on your head." I ignored the comment. I could spot verbal manipulation and I was having none of Dodge's.

Dash and Lil darted out from under the bed to greet me. Their coifs were stunning. It seemed obvious to me that one would take the ribbon for first place and the other would be runner-up. But, of course, I was prejudiced. Then a terrible thought occurred to me. If the letter writer so wanted to win this show such that he or she would stop at nothing, were Dash and Lil safe from some sort of foul play? I shuddered at the thought. Then I asked Dodge his thoughts on the subject.

"Are you fucking serious?" he said.

"Not in front of the cats!" I demanded. "There are four

hundred thousand words in the English language, Mr. Dodge. Certainly you can find suitable synonyms whilst in their presence."

Dodge exhaled and shook his head from side to side. He patted his stomach a few times. He closed his tired brown eyes, and rubbed his graying temples with his other hand. He was Rodan's *Thinker* with a headache and indigestion.

"Okay, Maybach," he said, as if defeated. "We'll play it your way. That bullet was really meant for you, not the widow. Fine. This whole thing really *is* about a cat show. Fine. Your cats are in great peril. Fine."

"There would be less of a need for your sarcasm, Mr. Dodge, if your message was a bit more consistent. If you don't believe any of this to be true, why did you say those very things to Bryce?" I asked.

"Because Bryce is a blabbermouth," Dodge said. "I can say 'blabbermouth' in front of the kitties, right?"

"I'm not following you."

"Bryce gets a drink into him and he loosens up. He tells anyone he sees what he knows. Eventually it will get back to the letter writer, right?"

"Yes."

"You think I want the letter writer to know that I'm onto his little scheme?"

"What scheme?"

"I don't know yet. But I sure as heck do know that it's got nothing to do with the cat show."

I thanked Dodge for showing restraint by using the word "heck" and then politely disagreed with him. He was an outsider here. He didn't understand the significance of the cat show. Part of the Judge's purging of the Salem curse was to embrace the symbol of the cat, as his ancestors believed that cats were minions of witches and agents of the Devil. Some were actually condemned based on the evidence of merely owning a cat. The

Judge believed that by instituting a cat show, and honoring those members of the town with the most "enchanting" cats, he'd be undoing the wrongs perpetrated by his kin. He believed that by living by their moral code while eviscerating their deadly superstitions, he would thereby undo the curse placed upon his family. Ultimately, he used one superstition to subdue another. Each year, since it was instituted, the cat show took place on the first of June—the anniversary of when the ordinance took effect for the town of Olde Sayville to go dry. And ever since that day, the curse appeared to have been lifted. One could question it all one liked, but it didn't matter. The people of the town all believed in it; ultimately that was all that mattered as it undeniably created a motive. But when I explained this to Dodge, he responded by laughing in my face.

"That's a very nice story, Monty. Maybe you should think about pitching it to Hollywood. Except, of course, you'll need to change the cats to T. Rexes, and the Judge to a big-breasted model in a wet t-shirt."

"Amazing how you can just dismiss hundreds of years of historical evidence, just because you're too narrow to think about the possibility that a curse can be real."

"I already know all there is to know about curses, my friend," Dodge shot back. "I've been a goddamn Rangers fan all my life. Now you think you could drive me to Elizabeth Hathorne's place? Cuz if you keep me here one more second, I'm going to feel obliged to sniff out your wine, and help myself to it."

"Think you know everything, don't you?" I said derisively. "No point in telling you anything. You refuse to learn. Out of spite. Let's go, Mr. Dodge. You grow tiresome."

"Finally, we see eye to eye," he retorted.

Our verbal sparring was interrupted by the telephone. It was Bryce calling, and he was hysterical. I reassured him and told him I was on my way.

"On your way where?" Dodge asked.

"Bryce's house," I said. "Gaston is missing."

"Who's that?" Dodge asked. "His butler?"

"No, you fool. His cat!"

"Jesus Christ," Dodge said. "You people have to get a grip. So you think the letter writer stole it? If you just put out some cat food, I'll bet you it'll find its way back."

"I'll take that wager," I said. "You see, whoever stole the cat left a ransom note."

🐾 🐾 🐾

BRYCE AND LYDIA DANFORTH WERE BOTH FRANTIC when Dodge and I arrived. Gaston, their Maine Coon, had been plucked from their home. Dodge grabbed the ransom note first, largely due to his lack of manners, and when he finished reading it he handed it to me. It read:

> *If E.H. won't play ball, the FIELD will need to be narrowed. May the last CAT standing win. Unless you'd rather PERSUADE her. Then you'll see Gaston much sooner, and in much LIVELIER SPIRITS.*

The poisoned pen writer had struck again. At that particular moment, I was very relieved that I made sure to double-lock the door to my hotel room before I left. Even though I believed Dash and Lil were clever little kitties and could take care of themselves, the extra sense of security was comforting.

"When did you find this note, Bryce?" I asked.

"When I got home; a couple of minutes before I called you."

"Where were you, Lydia?"

"I wasn't home yet," she said, trying to hold back her tears. "If only I hadn't played that extra set of tennis . . ." She broke off crying, and immediately reached for a tissue.

"Why should that matter?" Dodge asked.

"Well," she sobbed, "If I hadn't allowed Lloyd to talk me into that last set, I would have been home earlier and might have prevented it from happening." She dabbed at her eyes with the tissue, expertly preventing her makeup from running.

"How do you know when it happened?" Dodge asked. "If someone was going to snatch the cat, they'd have planned it when you'd normally be out of the house. I'd bet your cat was taken while you were playing your first set today."

Bryce rubbed his wife's sun-tanned shoulder. "See, I told you not to blame yourself, darling," he said. There was an uncomfortable silence after that. Dodge broke it.

"By the way," he said to Lydia, "I don't believe we've met. Phil Dodge, at your service." He extended his hand. Lydia cautiously, but nevertheless, politely offered her hand. Dodge immediately pulled the hand to his slobbering lips and placed a kiss upon it.

"Enchanté," he said with a bad French accent. Then Dodge grabbed me forcibly by the shoulder and pulled me toward the door.

"Have no fear. Maybach and I are on the case," he said. "But now Monty needs to drive me to Elizabeth Hathorne's residence. I do believe she will require a great deal of guarding tonight."

"I'll call her and let her know you're on your way," Bryce offered. Lydia sighed. Dodge pushed me harder toward the door, but I refused to budge. Bryce had been acting strangely all day and I wanted to talk to him—in private.

"Actually," I said, "I'd like to ask Bryce a few questions about this first, if I may."

"I really think we should be going, Monty," Dodge said through clenched teeth. We were having our first standoff and I refused to cede my position. I placed my hand in my pocket and firmly held onto my car keys, so as not to fall victim to another one of Dodge's automobile heists. And I held my ground. So much so, that through my power of suggestion, Dodge ended up enlisting Lydia to drive him to the Hathorne estate instead of me. As soon as the door closed behind them, I felt a sense of triumph. Not only was I rid of Dodge, I was now alone with Bryce.

"Have you eaten?" I asked him.

"No, not yet," he answered. Very distant.

"Why don't you let me whip something up for you? Then we can discuss the case over a nice meal."

Bryce nodded his assent. "All right," he said. "I'll give Elizabeth a quick call while you're in the kitchen."

As I entered the kitchen, I quickly scanned my memory for a recipe that would easily loosen one's lips. Being a gourmet chef had its advantages; especially when gathering information was on the menu.

7.
Dodge: A Slight Detour

LYDIA DANFORTH WAS A LOOKER. When I gawked at her through Bryce's office window, I was so enamored of her chest that I never noticed she had a great set of legs—showing off a pair of tight calves that she exhibited both on and off the tennis court. Right now, they nicely complemented the light tan leather seat of the roomy Lexus we were riding in. She was still wearing her tennis clothing, highlighted by a short little skirt, and she looked damn good in it. A hint of her perspiration lingered in the air, and I found it enticing.

"Do you play a lot of tennis, Mr. Dodge," she asked me.

"Why do you assume I play tennis, Mrs. Danforth?"

"Call me Lydia. Bryce's mother is the only Mrs. Danforth."

"And how do you get along with your mother-in-law?"

"Fabulously. She was long dead before I ever met Bryce." She smiled and we exchanged a laugh. I was on flirtation autopilot again. She grabbed the polished wooden knob on the stick shift and changed gears.

"But to answer your first question," she continued, "the reason that I assume you play tennis, Mr. Dodge . . ."

"Phil," I offered. She smiled.

"Well, Phil," she said, "you *are* wearing tennis whites, and tennis shoes."

She looked me up and down, then fingered the stick shift

again, although for no reason related to driving, and returned her focus to the road. Night was beginning to fall. I didn't want to tell her that the most time I'd ever spent on a tennis court was to dig it up to find a long-lost corpse that was mixed in with the cement.

"Well, Lydia," I said, "you must know that this get-up is nothing more than a costume."

She pulled on the stick and down-shifted before turning onto a dirt road. About half a mile in, she pulled off to the side and put the car in park, neatly nestled between two large shade trees.

"Perhaps we should remove the costume, then?" she said, advancing on me. "It seems so dishonest, don't you agree?"

She slid over toward me and placed a few kisses on my neck and began stroking my hair. I moved her mouth toward mine, and we sucked face for a few minutes. She reached for my belt buckle.

"You don't seem very concerned about your cat, do you?" I asked.

"It's Bryce's cat," she replied, and unbuckled my belt.

"I feel a little uncomfortable," I said.

"Let's move into the back seat, then. You won't have to worry about the stick shift."

"I'm not worried about that," I said.

"Then what's the problem?"

"Your husband hired me. He's technically my boss."

Lydia paused. She appeared to be deep in thought, but then proceeded to remove her shirt. My eyes almost leapt out of my head.

"I suppose that would make me the boss's wife, then. Technically speaking, of course."

"Of course," I agreed.

"And in the boss's absence, whatever I say goes, right?"

"I can't argue with your logic, Lydia," I said.

"Then shut up and take your pants off," she said lunging at me tongue first. As a conscientious employee, I couldn't refuse a direct order from a superior—especially a topless one.

* * *

LYDIA DANFORTH DIDN'T NEED ANY POINTERS when it came to sex, and she employed some rather creative techniques. However, during the highly enjoyable encounter, I found myself imagining that she was Elizabeth Hathorne instead. It was a silly fantasy I had—unlike Lydia, I knew a woman like Elizabeth could never bring herself down to the depths of my social class, and the fact that this was taking place in the back seat of a car just made the fantasy that much more absurd. But it sure as hell enhanced the entire experience. I held Lydia for a few minutes afterward, and then gently reminded her that we needed to get to Elizabeth Hathorne's home. Lydia bristled at the mention of the name.

"Of course," she said. "After all, I'm sure Bryce made damn sure to call and let her know we were on our way."

She adjusted her skirt and checked her hair. Then she put the car in gear and drove off.

"Does Bryce call Elizabeth often?" I asked.

Lydia sighed. She chose not to answer. But words weren't necessary. "Are she and Bryce having an affair?" I asked.

"Do you think I just screwed you because you're so damn appealing?" she lashed out, then started crying. It finally became clear to me. This had been a premeditated revenge fuck to get even with Bryce. And I was the lucky son of a bitch on the receiving end.

"I'm sorry, Lydia," I said. "I shouldn't have pried. I guess I'm just a little amazed is all. I mean, how could Bryce possibly see anything in the Hathorne widow, when you run circles around her in every way, shape and form?" A little white lie. It was the least I could do in exchange for the services she'd just provided. Lydia was sexy as hell—no doubt about it; but she wasn't in the same league as Elizabeth.

Through a cluster of tears, Lydia whispered "thank you, Phil." When we reached the Hathorne mansion, she told me she'd be happy to entertain me at any time during my visit in Olde Sayville. I gave her a long kiss and told her she could count on it. I got out of the car and headed up the cobblestone path to the front door. An arrangement with Lydia Danforth would certainly be mutually beneficial. She could pretend that I was Bryce, while I pretended that she was Elizabeth.

8.
Maybach: The Way to a Man's Secrets is Through His Stomach

BRYCE BEGAN TO SETTLE DOWN a bit when the appetizers were ready. Despite limited resources, I was still able to whip up platters of *Artichoke Bruschetta* and *Mushrooms Nicoise* without much difficulty. Until then, Bryce had been frustratingly tight-lipped and overly eager to change the subject whenever I brought up the poisoned pen letters.

"What is it that you're afraid of, Bryce?" I asked him after he took his second mouthful.

Bryce looked at me confused. I elaborated.

"It's obvious that you're keeping something from me. Otherwise you never would have brought Dodge into this. Why can't you confide in me?"

"Oh, Monty," he said, all choked up. "It's just that . . . I'd never forgive myself if anything happened to you."

"Like what?"

Bryce didn't answer. His eyes told me everything I needed to know.

"Who else is at risk here, Bryce?"

"Everyone and everything having to do with the Olde Sayville Society. You're an outsider, Monty. I want to make sure it stays that way. The less you know . . ."

The sound of a car coming up the driveway interrupted

Bryce's warning. I looked out the window and saw Lydia pulling into the garage. I knew I had only moments to get more information from Bryce. It was important that Lydia not be present, as Bryce may have been shielding her as well. Despite outward appearances, Lydia was also an outsider in Olde Sayville. The official story is that Bryce met Lydia Wentworth while away at college, where they fell in love and eloped. There was never any formal wedding. Lydia never discusses the Wentworth family except to mention that they are all living in Europe these days. The official rumor floating around Olde Sayville is that the Wentworths are wanted by the F.B.I. for an assortment of illegal business dealings, which led them to flee to Europe where they could be closer to their Swiss bank accounts. That's the "official" rumor, anyway. The "unofficial" rumor is that Bryce impregnated a waitress named Linda Wojciehowski, and after a botched abortion, Linda was left scarred and no longer able to have children. Needing immediate medical attention after the back-alley butchering, Bryce checked her into the hospital under the name Lydia Wentworth. After her full recovery, they eloped and concocted a far less scandalous rumor to explain Lydia's heritage. Either way, Lydia was still considered an "outsider."

"No one will know that I'm on the case, Bryce," I said, urging him to take me into his confidence. "Dodge has been hired to handle it. It's the perfect distraction. Don't you see? I couldn't be in a more protected position."

Bryce nodded in agreement. The sound of a key in the door sabotaged his would-be confession. Lydia was entering at the worst possible moment.

"Meet me at the club tomorrow morning," Bryce said quickly.

"When?"

"Six. Don't be late, but don't be early either."

"Six in the morning? I guarantee you I won't be early." I

said.

"Just be on time, okay?" he pleaded.

"I can't believe I'm still in my sweaty tennis clothes," Lydia announced as she entered the room. "I'm going to take a quick shower before dinner. Are you joining us, Monty?"

What she meant to say, of course, was *Will you prepare the meal for us, Monty?*

"Only if you allow me to cook," I said charitably.

"Wonderful. And hopefully you'll be able to uncover the monster who took Gaston."

I had a feeling that Bryce already knew that information. As I chopped the scallions, I wondered whether Lydia knew as well. After the initial report that Gaston had gone missing, they both seemed to be taking it in stride. Very puzzling. And Lydia certainly took her time driving back and forth from Elizabeth's house—much longer than what one would anticipate the round trip should take. Perhaps she made a side-trip on the way back; and perhaps that side-trip pertained to Gaston. Needless to say, I had my suspicions, but I wouldn't be able to know for sure until my meeting with Bryce the next morning.

The smell of the scallions gave me a sense-memory of a case I solved back in Newton. I had prepared *ceviche* for a small wedding celebration. Among the compliments I received was from the best man, who said it was the best he'd ever tasted, and that he'd tasted a lot of it over the past few years. The father of the bride was found dead the next morning. When the autopsy revealed that the father of the bride had been poisoned by a plant extract found in the Iberian peninsular region, I knew that the best man was the culprit. The best man's admission to having tasted much authentic *ceviche* over the last few years led me to believe that he'd been to Spain, where the plant was easily attainable. The groom had enlisted his best friend (and best man) to murder his father-in-law, but not until he was legally bound to his daughter, such that half the inheritance would be rightfully his. It was Dash who had initially alerted me to it, when he swatted at the stalk of a scallion, allowing me to recall the *ceviche* conversation with the best man.

But no such revealing information was offered during this scallion-enhanced dinner with Lydia and Bryce. I decided to put my curiosity on hold and enjoyed an elegant meal with friends instead. But in the corner of my mind, I couldn't help but wonder what Dodge was doing.

9.
Dodge: Widow's Weeds

ELIZABETH HATHORNE was not only classically beautiful, she exuded style and grace. She wore a strapless gown accented by long white gloves that went up to her elbows. When I asked Wanda if they were expecting company, she just shook her head and told me Mrs. Hathorne always dressed this way. Eccentric? Sure. But it worked for her.

"Have you had supper, Mr. Dodge?" the widow asked.

"Call me Phil," I said.

"Yes, you did mention that earlier. You must forgive me. My brain is rather addled, what with the recent events."

"I haven't eaten," I said. "What did you have in mind?"

She nodded to Wanda, who immediately exited the room with a purpose.

"We'll dine at eight," she said looking at a grandfather clock that read seven. "That should give you enough time to dress for dinner."

I smiled politely. I realized my clothes were a bit disheveled from my romp with Lydia Danforth. I made a mental note to always appear well-groomed in Elizabeth Hathorne's presence.

"I'll go upstairs and change, then," I said. "Will we be meeting for cocktails prior to dinner?"

The widow forced a smile. "I'll see you at eight, then," she said and left the room without answering my question. I was having a hard time believing that she and Bryce Danforth could be having an affair. Maybe it was something that Lydia concocted to justify her own infidelity. But then again, it would explain why Bryce was always smiling.

I went to my room and dug through the closet in search of something appropriate to wear. I couldn't decide between a suit, a sports jacket or a tuxedo. I called down to Wanda on the intercom and asked her advice. She seemed genuinely amused by my request, then told me to wear the tuxedo and hung up. I pulled on the dinner costume. I'd worn rented tuxes before, but nothing like this. For one thing, it had no ready-tied bowtie. I called Wanda again. She slogged up to my room to assist and got to work on it right away. She straightened the tie and pulled it gently to make sure it was the proper length on each side before she started to make the knot. The vastness of the old mansion, combined with Wanda's hunched posture, reminded me of an old Frankenstein movie—she was helping the "master" to dress up the "monster" that would ultimately never be able to fit in with their society.

"Sorry to impose on you, Wanda," I said.

"Not a problem," she said. She blew a wisp of gray hair from her face, while her hands continued to work on the knot. "I used to tie Judge Hathorne's bowtie every day, Mr. Dodge."

"Please, call me Phil," I said.

"Thank you, Mr. Dodge, but I'm not allowed to call any guests by their first name. Judge Hathorne was very particular about that."

I looked around, then whispered, "I promise I won't tell him." Then I chuckled. Wanda didn't take kindly to my little joke and nearly choked me with the bowtie. When she finished tying it, she curtly excused herself and closed the door loudly behind her.

I looked in the mirror at the creature in the monkey suit. You could dress up the pauper all you wanted, but it didn't make him a prince. And sometimes, that's the point. I hearkened back to my high school days. I was a city kid from Hell's Kitchen, living in the shadow of the old Madison Square Garden (which was largely responsible for my fanatical devotion to the New York Rangers). And I was extremely rough around the edges—I'm Emily fucking Post now compared to what I was then. This particular year, the Rangers had broken my heart, yet again, but not because they didn't win the Cup—I was used to that already. This time they did it by trading away Andy Bathgate, my favorite player, and childhood idol. In protest, I boycotted the rest of that pitiful hockey season (which turned out pretty well for Andy Bathgate—he won the Stanley Cup with the Maple Leafs). In lieu of hockey, I ended up developing a fascination with girls— especially rich girls. I'd cut school and jump the subway turnstile to take the train to the last stop in the Bronx, then walk uphill for a mile or so to hang out near the Fieldston School—a place where wealthy parents sent their kids to avoid having them exposed to the public school riff-raff represented by yours truly. So, I brought the seedy element to them—I made house calls. And I fell in love, or whatever passes for falling in love to a teenager. I had a secret affair with an enchanting redhead, who, for legal reasons, shall remain nameless. (Suffice it to say, her daddy was, and still is, a very powerful and influential man.)   After a few months of fooling around (nothing too unseemly—this was still prior to the free-love movement, yet another example of my piss-poor timing), she asked me to accompany her to her senior prom, and arranged for a limo and a tuxedo rental for me. Imagine the sight of a bunch of poor kids using brooms as makeshift hockey sticks slapping a roll of tape into an upended garbage can; then picture one of them wearing a tuxedo. That was me. I wore the tuxedo around Hell's Kitchen the entire day, showing off to my friends like I was someone important. What can I say, I was a dumb kid. The redhead wanted me to meet her family. Being a cocky kid, I thought I could pull it off, even though I had no clue how the other half lived. I slicked back my hair, and slapped on some of my grandfather's after shave, figuring that would make me appear more regal. But they could smell poor on me before I even made it through the door. And to their credit, they were very courteous to me. We left for the prom without incident, but we never made it there. A cop car intercepted the limo. There was some sort of "family emergency" and she needed to return home immediately. Translation: Her parents were mortified at the thought of their little princess being seen in public, let alone photographed for posterity, with the likes of me. The limo brought her back home, while a pair of cops gave me a lift back to Hell's Kitchen. I also got a lecture on the ways of the world. "Guys like you and me," one cop said, "we're just not in that league, son. So take my advice and just back off. There are plenty of girls in your own neighborhood." But I was in love, I told him, and love cannot be denied. Next thing I remember was my grandfather taking me home from the precinct. Granted, I was just a dumb kid speaking from his heart, but that was no reason to force-feed me whiskey and arrest me for public drunkenness. It was my word against not one, but two of New York's Finest, and since I was a minor, as well as a first-time offender, it was easier to just plead it out. A couple of days later, the redhead called me. I told her I was sorry that she had to miss her senior prom, just because of me. But here's the kicker—the limo never returned the redhead home. It took her straight to the prom where her father had a date arranged and waiting for her. Apparently, he was prepared for it because the previous year, she brought home some poor schmuck from Astoria for her junior prom. His little girl, it seemed, had an appetite for riff-raff and loved to flaunt it in her rich daddy's face. She told me all about the ballroom, and the dancing, and the prime rib that I missed. Still impetuous and "in love," I asked if we could meet in secret. She said she didn't really want to see me any more. The actual reason for her call was to remind me to return the tuxedo, because it was a day overdue. And now it's thirty years overdue. If I ever fall in love again, maybe I'll return it.

I looked at my watch—it was ten minutes to eight. Maybe, just maybe, there would be a secret pre-dinner cocktail waiting for me. I adjusted my ill-fitted tuxedo, and began my trek down to the dining room. I rubbed my stomach. The tiny gymnast was practicing somersaults on my pancreas. I made a mental note to find myself another doctor.

✳ ✳ ✳

THERE WERE NO PRE-DINNER COCKTAILS. My gastro-enteral acrobat and I were seated at the dining room table at exactly eight o'clock. The dinner conversation was polite but awkward. I felt so ill-at-ease in front of the widow; not only because of our difference in class, but due to the fact that the waist of my tuxedo pants was about an inch too small. I had to leave the pants unbuttoned, and hope that the cummerbund would cover it. But the game of dress-up wasn't the only thing causing me discomfort. I was also suffering from an uncharacteristic case of clumsiness. I'd drop my silverware, while worrying whether I was using the right spoon for the right course. But Elizabeth was the personification of icy elegance. And she never even removed her elbow-length gloves the whole time.

"I hope the prime rib isn't too rare for you, Phil," she said. "I prefer my meat red and juicy." She lifted a particularly bloody piece on her fork and popped it in her mouth. As I watched her, my dirty mind took over. I imagined her dining there naked, wearing nothing but the gloves, until my cummerbund started to move. Then I accidentally knocked over my water glass. Wanda did not hide her dissatisfaction at having to wipe up my spill. Why was I acting this way? Like an immature schoolboy with a crush on his hot, but utterly unattainable homeroom teacher?

"Shall we retire to the parlor for coffee and dessert, Phil?" she asked.

"As you wish, Elizabeth." I carefully stood up and followed her to the parlor.

I sat in a chair a few feet away from her, with my legs crossed, so as not to arouse too much suspicion around my ventilated trousers. To illuminate the room, Wanda placed a large candelabra behind Elizabeth's chair. The flames flickered and danced about, casting unusually long shadows, but I wasn't distracted by them—I couldn't take my eyes off Elizabeth. I was entranced by the beautiful shapes that her lips made when she spoke. We made small talk, until Elizabeth finally changed the subject to the poisoned pen letter. She wanted to know if I'd made any progress on the case and if I'd uncovered anything.

"Bryce made it pretty clear to me that I should let the police handle that end of it," I said. "I'm really more of a bodyguard than anything else."

"So you'll take the first bullet, and I'll take the second? That doesn't seem like a very good plan." She shifted in the chair, arched her back and gazed sadly out the window. But instead of watching her now-pouting lips, I was distracted by the long shadow that her pert breasts were casting across my lap.

"What do you think the motive is?" I asked trying to stay focused on the conversation.

"To discredit me. Or maybe to tarnish my late husband's memory. If I'm not firm in my resolve—if I am made to look like a coward—the Hathorne family name will be irreparably harmed."

"Then you shouldn't be worried about a murder attempt," I said. "If the letter writer's intention is to bring shame upon you, certainly he or she wouldn't want to make a martyr out of you."

She shifted back toward me and shook her head. "Unfortunately," she said, "I can't be certain of that." The shadows across my lap were now that of her head moving from side to side; and the flickering, dancing flames in the candelabra behind her created the illusion of her head's shadow bobbing up and down on my crotch. It was at that moment that I decided to try and patch things up with God. I petitioned Him, and prayed that this shadowing become a foreshadowing (or a "foreplay-shadowing," as it were) of things to come. If He could deliver this most impossible of acts, it would be on the order of a miracle. But in the meantime, my frustration was building, and my head was about to explode. I resolved that an early morning visit with Lydia Danforth was in order—she could provide a tension release.

"How did you meet your husband?" I asked, squirming in my seat, trying to think about anything else.

"I was in college at the time. Doing a research paper on the descendants of Salem," she said with a smile, totally oblivious to my situation. "I just fell in love with him during the interview."

"Weren't you even a little bit afraid of marrying him—because of the curse, I mean?"

"That was fifteen years earlier. Everyone thought that the curse had been extinguished at that point. But I suppose it was only in remission—it's finally caught up with me."

Her smile faded as our eyes locked. She leaned forward and touched my hand with her white satin glove. The mere touch sent a warm tingle down my spine. "Please," she whispered. "Find the person who's writing these letters. You're my only hope."

I held her gloved hand, resisting my urge to stroke it. "I'll do everything in my power," I said.

The indication of a tear began to form around her left eye. She was trying extremely hard not to cry; or at least trying to make it look that way. I took the bait and patted her hand. "There, there," I said. "I won't let anything bad happen to you."

"Thank you," she said, composing herself. She squeezed my hand. "My life is in your hands."

The warm tingle down my spine transformed into a chilling shiver. I removed my hand from her grip, reassured Elizabeth that I would protect her, and abruptly excused myself, declaring that I needed to retire for the evening.

Lying awake in the guest room, I stared up at the ceiling. Her words haunted me: "My life is in your hands." This scene was becoming far too reminiscent of a case I had twenty years earlier. Her name was Valerine Rizzo—a six-foot blonde with a lazy eye. She was looking to reclaim some jewelry that her ex-husband had made off with, even though the divorce settlement specifically awarded said jewels to Ms. Rizzo. She hired me to find the guy and collect the merchandise—by any means necessary. Normally, I could tell if a case was on the level just by staring the potential client in the face. But her lazy eye wandered all over my office, and I couldn't quite tell for sure. I took on the case anyway. Hell, I needed the money. And even if it wasn't on the level, what harm was there? Two weeks into the case, I still hadn't turned up any leads on the husband, but I had successfully made my way into Valerine's bed. That was my style back then. Seducing the clientele was my favorite pastime. We went out for drinks one night, presumably to discuss the case. True to form, the discussion went the way of flirtation. During our innuendo-filled chat, I asked her about her name, since I had never met anyone named Valerine before. As it turned out, her parents wanted to name her Valerie, but the typist accidentally added an "n" when typing up the birth certificate. Her parents thought it was cute, so the name "Valerine" stuck. "I guess that means you're one of a kind," I told her in unabashed cheeseball form. I remember her response vividly: "You'll never meet another one like me," she said. "This is your one and only shot at a Valerine." The lure was irresistible. An hour later, we were naked.

Later that week, in a moment of post-coital bliss, Valerine said that when I finally did find her husband that I should be extra careful. When I asked her why she'd chosen this moment in particular to warn me, and why she'd waited so long to parlay this looming siren of danger, she simply replied: "My life is in your hands." We never did subscribe to the standard run-of-the-mill pillow talk.

I continued to stare up at the ceiling in the guest bedroom at the Hathorne mansion, refusing to fall asleep. Because I knew once I did, I'd dream about Valerine. I'd dream about the day I had to identify her remains.

10.
Maybach: An Early Exit

DASH AND LIL LOOKED AT ME as if I were out of my mind. Where on earth could I be going at this ungodly hour? They remained snuggled around their pillows, and didn't offer to bid me *adieu* at the door like they usually did. I wiped the crust from my eyes and headed to the hotel parking lot. There was no attendant on duty at this hour, so I walked up the ramp and huffed and puffed my way to my car. I popped the trunk and partook in some chocolate pleasure before my departure.

When I arrived at the club, Bryce's was the lone car in the lot. I gave my face a few polite slaps to get my blood circulating. I needed to be fully awake when I spoke to Bryce. I looked at my watch—it was six a.m. exactly. I was neither early, nor late, just as Bryce had requested. The scene was strikingly familiar to the first time I'd met Bryce—when I was interviewing for the catering assignment for the Judge and Elizabeth's anniversary banquet. My dear friend, Geoffrey, had arranged it for me. I remember making this very walk, filled with nervous energy, checking my watch to make sure I was exactly on time to make a good impression. Bryce was all smiles then, in stark contrast to the troubled man I saw last night. I got the job, of course, and right after the banquet, Bryce told me that, while he couldn't have been happier with my performance, it was Geoffrey who had tipped the scales in my favor, by promising to write an article about the event in his syndicated column. Geoffrey, to this day, has never told me about it, and I have never let on that I know what he did for me. The only other keeper of that secret was Bryce Danforth, who was now in dire need of my assistance. I felt myself trembling a bit as I walked from the parking lot to the club's entrance—I was far more nervous now than I was for the interview.

When I got to the office door, I gave myself another polite slap and proceeded to knock; but there was no response—no human response, that is. Through the door I heard a feline's loud caterwauling. I twisted the handle and pushed the door open. To my utter surprise, a frightened and disoriented Gaston was standing on a toppled wheelchair in the middle of the room. There was blood on his paws and he was meowing his lungs out. And lying face down on the floor next to the wheelchair was a very dead Bryce Danforth. A bloody marble bust of the Judge lay on the floor beside Bryce's crushed skull. A five-word typewritten note was prominently featured on the desk. *"THESE ARE NOT IDLE THREATS."*

If only I'd arrived early—perhaps I could have prevented this. I crouched down and touched his arm. Cold. He appeared to have been dead for a while. Poor Bryce—not without his flaws, but not without his charm. He didn't deserve this. I vowed then and there that I would find the killer. But I knew I couldn't do it alone. I grudgingly reached for the phone.

Calmly, and with great resolve, I made two calls. First I telephoned the police, and told the young officer on early morning desk duty that a murder had been committed. Then I called Elizabeth Hathorne's home. Wanda answered.

"So sorry to wake you, Wanda dear," I said.

"You didn't wake me," she said. "I'm always up early."

"If he's not yet awake, I was wondering if you could rouse Mr. Dodge. If it's not too much trouble, that is."

"No trouble at all," she said. "It'll be my pleasure."

Dodge came to the phone a few minutes later.

"This better be good," a cracked, hoarse voice said without even saying 'hello' first.

"You'd better get down to the club," I said. "Bryce is dead. I just found him. Another note as well."

"Have you called the police?"

"Yes. Just a few minutes ago."

"I better hurry then," he said. "What about his wife, have you called her?"

"Not yet," I said.

"Well, don't. Let the cops handle that. And for Christ's sake, don't touch anything!"

Then he abruptly hung up without even saying 'goodbye.'

Gaston rubbed up against my leg. I lifted the scared, affection-starved cat and cradled him in my arms, while I scanned the room. Aside from the bloody bust on the floor, and the overturned wheelchair, nothing else was out of place— indicating that there probably wasn't much of a struggle. Bryce likely never saw it coming.

Gaston began to meow again—as if he were crying for his slain daddy.

"There, there," I whispered to him. "I'll find out who did this. You can count on it."

11.
Dodge: Breaking News

I ENLISTED BRIGGS, the Hathorne family chauffeur, to drive me to the club. Elizabeth was still asleep and Wanda refused to wake her up. I made Wanda promise me that she wouldn't say anything to Elizabeth until I got back. I wanted to break the news to her myself about Bryce's death. If she and Bryce were having an affair and Lydia knew about it, then statistically speaking, that automatically made both of them suspects. I seriously doubted either of them being capable of it, but being an experienced P.I., I also knew that the numbers didn't lie. I needed reassurance that they were both snug in their beds when the homicide occurred. But first I had to get to the crime scene to determine exactly when the murder took place before the police got there and contaminated all the evidence.

"How was your day off, Briggs?" I asked, just to make small talk and keep both of us awake.

"Uneventful, sir."

And that was the transcript of our entire conversation.

The predictably tardy police still hadn't arrived when we pulled into the club's driveway. Only Maybach's Mercedes and Bryce's Lexus were in the parking lot. I told Briggs not to wait for me and I jumped out of the car before he could get out and open the door for me. I felt uncomfortable making another person work to do something so pointless. And since there was no one around to blow my cover, there was really no need for the pretense. I moved quickly into the club and navigated my way to Bryce's office. Maybach was waiting for me outside the office door. He was holding a cat in his arms.

"What's with the cat?" I asked.

"Meet Gaston. I found him in the room with Bryce."

"Let's go in."

He opened the door for me and we entered the room. Bryce was dead all right. I carefully walked around the upended wheelchair, leaned down and touched his left hand. Cold. And rigid. I checked his right hand. A little less rigid. Upon closer inspection, I noticed that the fingers on his right hand were broken.

"Where does the sculpture usually go?" I asked Maybach.

"The desk, I believe."

I walked off eight paces from Bryce's body to the desk. I saw the note. *"THESE ARE NOT IDLE THREATS."*

"Have you ever held that thing?" I asked, pointing at the Judge-turned-murder weapon.

"I have, in fact."

"How much do you figure it weighs?" I asked him.

"Well, I couldn't say for certain."

"I'm not asking you to say for certain. I'm asking you to make a guess. Ten pounds? Twenty pounds?"

"Ten pounds sounds about right. Possibly a little more. Possibly a little less."

I reached for my camera, but realized, in my sleep-deprived early morning daze, I'd forgotten to bring it. I cursed myself and then stuck my face in the crushed portion of Bryce's skull. The smell was pretty bad, but it was also pretty early so luckily my olfactory senses hadn't fully kicked in yet. The injuries sustained seemed to indicate that Bryce received multiple blows to the head. I wanted to try to get a whiff of Bryce's breath, but there was no way I could without moving the body. It may have been possible that he was actually sitting in the wheelchair when he was attacked, and then unceremoniously dumped out of it. And, seeing as I had already witnessed him using it as a drinking chair, it would explain why he may not have heard anyone sneak up on him. I stood up and walked over to the giant portrait of the Judge. I moved the picture to reveal the safe. It was locked.

"You know the combo for this?" I asked.

"Of course not. Why would I?"

There was no way, at the moment, to check if any more Scotch was missing from the decanter, which means I would have to depend on the cops and the toxicology reports. I returned the portrait back to its original position, then turned to Maybach.

"Last question, Maybach. What the hell were you doing here?"

"Bryce asked me to meet him here. He was going to reveal some information pertinent to the case."

"Who else knew about this?"

"No one that I know of. Possibly Lydia, but that would be about it."

I heard a siren. The overdue police were finally arriving. Simultaneously, Maybach and I looked at our watches.

"Thirty-seven minutes," Maybach said, shaking his head. "Inexcusable."

"Maybe they got held up at the donut shop," I countered.

"Not in this town," Maybach answered. "They have all their meals catered."

I peered out through the Venetian blinds and saw two officers lackadaisically getting out of a police car. I turned back to Maybach.

"Seeing as you discovered the body," I said, "you're gonna have to stick around for a while and tell them everything you know. How 'bout you lend me your car for an hour or so?"

"Lend?"

"It doesn't really matter what you say, Monty. I'm gonna take it no matter what. I just thought I'd ask first. It's a tad more civilized this way."

"Fine," he groaned and handed me his car keys.

"I'll be back as soon as I can," I said and headed out. I greeted the police officers when I got outside and told them that Maybach was waiting inside for them. I also suggested that they check out Bryce's car, as it might hold some clues as to what he was doing there so early. I doubted they would find anything, but I wanted to keep them busy. Then I hopped into the Mercedes and hit the gas.

* * *

"WHAT A PLEASANT SURPRISE," Lydia Danforth said when she greeted me at the door. She was wearing a skimpy little robe that showed off her assets to perfection.

"I hope I didn't wake you," I said.

"It is rather early, isn't it?" she replied. "But your timing is excellent. Bryce probably won't be home for hours." Then she pulled me inside, shut the door, clasped her arms around my neck and stuck her tongue down my throat. Within seconds, her robe had fallen by her feet. I was torn about how to proceed. After all, I had planned on a quick morning romp with Lydia, while being nearly teased to death by Elizabeth's shadow the night before. I tossed an imaginary coin, and it came up tails. I grudgingly asked Lydia to put her robe back on.

"Then why are you here?" she asked practically spitting. "So you can tell me you prefer Elizabeth Hathorne, too?"

I tried to gently stroke her hair, but she would have none of it.

"Don't you fucking touch me, you Neanderthal."

"I need to talk to you about Bryce," I said, forcing my way into the one-sided conversation.

"And that takes precedence over a naked woman kissing you?"

"Lydia," I said, "do you seriously think I would turn down this kind of action unless I had a damn good reason? I need to ask you a few questions. This isn't a social call—it's business."

"Well, I don't feel much like talking right now," she said. "Come back during business hours."

"Lydia . . ."

"I think you should go now, Mr. Dodge."

"What time did Bryce leave this morning?" I asked, ignoring her request.

"I don't know. I was probably asleep. Please leave."

"Well, then maybe you could narrow it down for me. When did you first notice that he'd slipped out of bed?"

"How the hell should I know?" she screamed as the crying episode began. "We haven't slept in the same room, let alone the same bed in months." She heaved as she wept. "Why don't you ask Elizabeth when he slipped out of her bed?" Then she charged me, swinging her arms and punching.

"God, I hate you. All of you."

I grabbed Lydia's arm and twisted it behind her back. She was screaming and flailing—totally hysterical. I twisted her arm harder, and flipped her around so I could look her right in the eyes. She spit in my face, so I slapped hers in exchange. She gasped, shocked that I would do such a thing.

"You're no gentleman," she screeched.

"No shit," I answered, and slapped her again. This one finally produced the desired effect—it got her to shut up for five seconds so I could speak.

"Bryce is dead."

I felt her body tense up, then slowly relax. She turned her head and stared toward the window, dreamlike.

"Yes," she said quietly. "Of course he is."

12.
Maybach: The Cat's Meow

GASTON DIDN'T APPEAR TO BE HARMED in any way by his captor. He was disoriented, but that was most likely from being in a strange place. There were a few drops of dried blood matted to his fur. Despite Gaston's meowed protestations, I combed them out as best as I could. Bryce would have wanted it that way.

The adolescent in the police uniform grilled me at length as to the reason for my early arrival at the club, and ended the interview by warning me not to leave Olde Sayville. "Perish the thought," I told the lad. "If I were to leave, how on earth would the murderer be brought to justice?" He didn't take kindly to my cutting remark.

As he had promised, Dodge returned shortly thereafter and, at his request, we drove to Elizabeth's house. On the way there, I saw Chip Danforth in his yellow Lamborghini speed past us in the opposite direction.

"I guess he just found out about his uncle," I said.

"I guess," Dodge replied, unfazed.

"I wonder how Lydia is taking the news," I offered.

Dodge didn't respond. He just kept his sleepy brown eyes fixed straight ahead as we turned onto the private road leading to the Hathorne estate. Wanda was waiting for us by the door.

"May I get you something to eat or drink, Mr. Maybach?" she asked, with a matronly smile.

"Thank you, but no," I said. The morning's escapades had killed my appetite. I briefly thought about writing a diet book, *Shed the Pounds: Discover a Dead Body*, but even I found that to be in poor taste.

"I wouldn't mind a little breakfast, Wanda," Dodge said.

"Well, you know where it is, Mr. Dodge," she snapped, as her smile faded into oblivion. "Help yourself." She turned on her heels and walked away. I was immediately taken aback, as I'd never witnessed Wanda being anything less than cordial.

"Making friends everywhere you go, I see," I said, relishing the opportunity to toss a barb Dodge's way.

"How was I supposed to know she was boffing the Judge?" he replied. I stared at him dumbfounded.

"Surely, you jest!" I exclaimed when I finally found my voice.

"Yeah," he said. "I guess you just don't get my big city sense of humor around here."

Thankfully, Elizabeth entered the room before I had to endure any more of Dodge's alleged hilarity. She brought with her a very worried look. Elizabeth's normally cool and level demeanor was not present today.

"I heard about Bryce," she said. "Is it really true?"

"I'm afraid so," I answered.

"Who told you?" Dodge asked.

"Wanda," she replied.

Dodge muttered something under his breath. Most certainly it was a vulgar phrase, but thankfully, unintelligible. Elizabeth suggested we move into the parlor. Her slender legs seemed to be a bit wobbly. I took her hand to escort her, but Dodge interrupted.

"I think we should all go down to the club," he said. "How long will it take for you to get ready, Elizabeth?"

Elizabeth's eyes widened, and her face dropped. She had a pained expression.

"I'm ready now, Phil. Why? Don't I look all right?"

"You look exquisite," I said, trying to counteract Dodge's inadvertent *faux pas.*

"You sure do," added Dodge. He looked her up and down—I thought he was going to start drooling at any moment. Elizabeth was a striking woman, and kept herself in excellent physical shape. Still, for some strange reason, she seemed uncertain and highly self-conscious about her appearance—or, more precisely, what Dodge thought of her appearance. I leapt to the rescue.

"You just may want to consider wearing something with short sleeves," I said. "It's unseasonably warm out there."

"But I feel so cold right now," she said. "I've been shivering all morning."

Dodge brazenly put his arm around her, rubbed her shoulders and escorted her out the door, down the path and into the waiting limousine. I briefly exchanged glances with Briggs after he shut the door. He emitted a tiny shrug, then got behind the wheel and drove off. I doubt that Dodge or Elizabeth even bothered to notice if I was following or not.

⚓ ⚓ ⚓

THE CLUB'S PARKING LOT was practically full when I drove in behind Elizabeth's limousine. Olde Sayville was a small community and word tended to travel rather quickly. There was an air of solemnity when we entered the club. We went directly to the office, where the police were in the process of removing Bryce's body. A few club members, Lydia Danforth among them, were huddled together, seated behind Bryce's desk, being interviewed by two officers. There weren't enough chairs to accommodate them all, so several other officers were scurrying about, bringing extra chairs into the office. In the meantime, Lydia Danforth was seated in the wheelchair.

"Are you fucking kidding me?" Dodge cried out.

13.
Dodge: Jokers Wild

NOBODY—AND I MEAN *NOBODY*—who'd spent even an hour at the police academy would allow a crime scene to be contaminated like that. The area was never sealed, no physical evidence was collected other than the body and the sculpture, and no attempt was made to preserve the scene, as people were now trudging in and out of the room. I asked if it would be possible for me to see the photographs of the body, only to be informed that none were taken. I ruled out gross incompetence immediately. It had to be intentional.

With no evidence other than what Maybach and I had initially discovered, I thought it best to conduct my own interviews. I grabbed Maybach so we could work the room. I needed someone to introduce me to people now that Bryce, my previous host, was permanently unavailable. The first person we found was the impassive Chip Danforth.

"How are you holding up, Chip?" Maybach asked. "We're all just so devastated by this."

"I'm kind of numb," he responded evenly. "I still can't believe it."

"When was the last time you spoke to your uncle?" I interjected.

"Yesterday, I guess," Chip answered. "When he introduced the two of us. I think that was the last time I saw him." Chip was not someone I would play poker with. There was nothing in his expression that gave anything away.

As I was formulating my next question, Lydia caught sight of us and joined our group. She and Chip embraced in a long, consoling hug. Then a hug from Monty. It wouldn't be appropriate for her to hug me in these circumstances—I guess there's a certain decorum about the way a high-society wife greets the last man she had sex with prior to her husband's murder—so, I just accepted her outstretched hand and offered words of condolence.

"Thank you for your support, Mr. Dodge," she said. "And I hope you will be able to bring the killer to justice."

"What are you talking about?" Chip chimed in immediately.

Lydia had just blown my cover.

"I'm a private detective," I conceded. "Your uncle hired me."

"Is that why you were asking me all those questions?" Chip asked indignantly, finally showing some emotion. "You think I killed my own uncle or something?"

"I just wanted to know when you saw him last. I'm trying to fill in a timeline," I explained.

"Well, if it's all the same to you, I don't think I'll be answering any more of your questions, Mr. Dodge." And Chip Danforth abruptly walked away. My eyes followed him as he walked over to Blake Giles, whispered something in his ear, and pointed in my direction. Giles emitted a look of surprise and immediately set off for another club member. More whispering and pointing ensued. I looked over at Lydia.

"Sorry," she said. "I wasn't thinking."

Somehow, I didn't buy her line. It seemed like my outing was premeditated. Perhaps it was her way of getting even with me for rejecting her advances earlier that morning. But now the damage was done and I needed to mitigate my losses quickly. I looked at Maybach. I hated what I was about to say. I took a deep breath and let loose.

"All right, Monty. No one's going to talk to me now, so I guess it's up to you. I need you to find out where every single person in this club was the last twelve hours, and the last time they saw or spoke to Bryce."

"I thought you'd never ask," he said, failing to suppress a smug grin, and then waddled off in victory.

"I guess that frees up some of your time," Lydia said after Monty left.

"Sorry I left so abruptly this morning," I said. "I didn't want to be there when the police came to tell you about Bryce."

"I understand," she said, though I doubt she meant it.

"I saw you talking to the cops when I walked in," I said. "What did you tell them?"

"The truth. I told them that I thought Elizabeth killed him."

I quickly scanned the room and saw Elizabeth talking to a cop.

"I think she's got a pretty rock-solid alibi, Lydia," I said. "I stayed at the house last night and nobody came or went the whole time." Of course, I wasn't at all certain of that. Even though I'd been awake, staring at the ceiling for most of the night, I was in a remote room in the house—it's quite possible that I wouldn't have heard people coming and going; especially if they didn't want to be heard.

"She may not have been the one that bashed his skull in," she conceded, tears beginning to stream from her eyes, "but it was because of her that it happened. Bryce took on the letter writer for her and wound up dead." High-society wife decorum be damned, she put her arms around me and hugged me tight. She needed comfort from me and she didn't care what anyone in the room saw or thought. I complied and hugged her right back. But through our embrace I couldn't help but wonder. If what Lydia said was true, then Bryce probably knew the identity of the letter writer, and was likely going to reveal it to Monty. Maybe Elizabeth knew as well.

✳ ✳ ✳

I THOUGHT IT BEST TO RETURN to the Hathorne estate as soon as Elizabeth completed her police interview. Before I left, Lydia made me promise that I'd visit her sometime that afternoon. I also said my goodbyes to Maybach, and asked him to swing by Elizabeth's house after he was done probing the members and gathering information.

Briggs drove us home and no one spoke for the first five minutes or so. Elizabeth appeared to have something on her mind, and I wanted to find out what it was. I broke the ice by asking her how the police interview went.

"You seemed rather friendly with Lydia Danforth," she said, not answering the question.

"Yes," I answered. "She was in need of some support and comfort, and I happened to be there to provide it."

"I see," she said. "Well, I'd like to set the record straight. That woman has been spreading vicious lies about me."

"Really? Like what?"

"She accused me of having an affair with Bryce."

So that's what was bothering her. I had no other choice but to challenge her.

"And did you?"

Elizabeth stared at me. The look on her face was one of total revulsion and disbelief.

"Of course not," she said indignantly. "How could you even suggest such a thing?" She began to pout.

Uncharacteristically, I quickly apologized. "It's just the nature of my work. I have to ask these questions. It's not my intention to upset you. Please forgive me."

Her look softened, as did her tone. "Of course, I forgive you, Phil. I'm sorry I lost my temper."

She began to rub her long sleeves against her arms.

"Are you still cold?" I asked.

"Terribly," she said.

I cautiously placed my arm around her and she shifted herself closer to me, presumably for warmth. She took hold of my hand, and began to absentmindedly stroke my fingers. I looked up and saw Briggs's bloodshot eyes staring back at me in the rearview mirror. I gave him a wink. He quickly shifted his focus to the road ahead. I returned my attention to the widow, who was now snuggled up against me.

"Thank you," she said. "I just know you'll protect me, won't you Phil?"

That triggered another memory of Valerine Rizzo. After a while, I stopped protecting Valerine—I merely saw her as a prize that I'd won, a six-foot blonde adornment on my arm. And it was that same dereliction of duty that led to six feet of bloodied pulp in a wooden box. I was older and supposedly wiser now. I vowed to myself that I wouldn't allow the same thing to happen to Elizabeth. No matter what.

"As if my life depended on it," I found myself saying.

Then she pushed a button on the back seat console and an opaque tinted partition ascended, completely isolating us from Briggs's prying eyes in the rearview mirror. Elizabeth stared intently at me—as if she needed to tell me something secret and urgent; but instead, she leaned in and kissed me. It wasn't a passionate kiss by any means, but it was more than a friendly peck on the lips.

"Thank you," she whispered. "You're a life-saver."

Just as I was about to grab her and kiss her right back, she pushed the button on the console and lowered the partition to its original position—Briggs's suspicious eyes stared back at me.

It was clear to me now that I had no control over myself when I was around Elizabeth. Even though I had resolved not to allow a repeat of the Valerine episode, I was a mere millisecond away from attempting to ravage Elizabeth right there in the back seat. What was it about her? Sure, she was beautiful, but so were a lot of other women I'd known. Hell, Lydia was a knockout, but

I didn't feel this way around her. Maybe it was the fact that I saw Elizabeth as completely unattainable. It reminded me of what those cops told me on my aborted prom date with the Redhead-who-will-remain-nameless: "She's out of your league, son." The similarities were there. Except that I was just a dumb kid who thought he was "in love" back then. I was older and wiser now.

14.
Maybach: The Proof is in the Pudding

I SAT IN A STALL in the Olde Sayville Society rest room and jotted down everything I'd just learned. No one could see me. No one would suspect me. I was now the lead investigator and I was going to make the most of it. And unlike Dodge, I would not allow my cover to be blown. After writing volumes of details about each and every club member that I'd interviewed—all in the guise of finding out their culinary preferences for the Olde Sayville gala banquet, I tucked my notepad away and drove directly to Elizabeth Hathorne's home.

The normally congenial Wanda was in a foul mood when I arrived. Phil Dodge can have that effect on people. I sympathized, as I'd experienced it first-hand. Wanda showed me to the parlor where Dodge was waiting for me.

"Where is Elizabeth?" I asked.

"Trying to get some rest. I talked her into taking a sleeping pill," he said. "She's still shivering and it sure as hell isn't cold in here."

"Poor thing. Probably a bad case of nerves is all."

"Thanks for the diagnosis, doctor," Dodge said facetiously.

"Shall we discuss the case?" I asked, taking the high road.

"Yeah, what'd you find out?"

I sat down on an arm chair and produced my notepad. I flipped it open and thumbed through it until I reached the first relevant page. I cleared my throat a few times, in preparation of reading aloud. Then Dodge ripped the pad from my hands, and began to hastily scan it on his own.

"You're not a very patient man, are you, Mr. Dodge?"

"Not when it comes to murder, Monty," he said and continued reading. "Who the hell is Quail? What was he wearing?"

"There is no one named Quail, Mr. Dodge. The Colonel prefers quail's eggs to *foi gras.*"

"Holy leaping shit, Maybach! I asked you to find out two fucking things—where they were the last twelve hours and the last time they saw Bryce."

I could take no more. I stood up and grabbed the notepad back from Dodge. I flipped through and came upon a page and then shoved it back into Dodge's face.

"Here," I said. "It's a chart with everyone's name and alleged alibi. The food topic was my way of starting a conversation and inconspicuously allowed me to take notes whilst speaking with them. Need I remind you of the importance of retaining one's cover story?"

Dodge gawked at the chart. Then he looked over to me.

"Nice work, Monty," he said. "Based upon these findings, the only ones here that don't have an eyewitness to verify their alibis are . . ."

"Chip Danforth, Blake Giles, Eliot Stoughton, Rudolf, and the Colonel," I finished his sentence for him.

"Don't forget Lloyd. And Lydia Danforth," Dodge added, handing the notepad back to me.

"Well, yes," I agreed. "But I didn't get to interview them. Lloyd wasn't there, but I would definitely count him among the suspects. Surely you don't suspect Lydia, though."

Dodge exhaled a deep sigh. "How can I not, Maybach?" he asked. He rubbed his eyes. He seemed genuinely saddened by this.

"You didn't sleep with her, did you?" I asked.

Dodge looked at me for a moment, then smiled. "I underestimated you, Monty. I guess you *have* got a big city sense of humor." His demeanor changed and his mood picked up.

"How about you give me a ride to the police station?" he said. "It's time we had a little talk with the top man over there."

We made our way to the front door. Wanda was there to bid us farewell. Then a thought crossed my mind.

"What about Elizabeth?" I asked. "Is it safe for her here all alone?"

"She'll be asleep for awhile," Dodge said. "Besides Wanda here will take good care of her, won't you Wanda?"

Wanda growled at Dodge. We headed down the path to my Mercedes. I popped the trunk and, as a peace offering, handed Dodge one of my special chocolates before we embarked on our big adventure. Dodge looked at it unenthusiastically, but, nonetheless, accepted it graciously. Once he bit into it, however, a great big grin sprouted across his face.

"Thanks, Monty," he said. "I needed that."

"You're welcome, Mr. Dodge."

"Please," he said, "call me, Phil."

15.
Dodge: A History Lesson

THE OLDE SAYVILLE POLICE STATION looked like a cross between an antiques shop and a bed and breakfast. A friendly officer/receptionist greeted us as Maybach and I entered, and cheerfully pointed us in the direction of the Chief of Police. We ambled into his office unannounced. The door was open, after all.

"Well, if it isn't Messrs. Maybach and Dodge," the Chief said as we approached, showing off that he knew who we were. I waited for him to stand up, only to realize he already was standing. The walls of the office were covered with framed newspaper clippings, and his desk was cluttered with little knick-knacks, and wind-up toys. There didn't appear to be enough room for the Chief to keep any sort of case files.

"We were wondering if we could have a little chat," I said. "Get to know each other better."

"Sure thing. I've got nothing better to do—'cept of course that pesky murder earlier today and the attempted murder from yesterday."

"We promise not to take up too much of your time," Maybach said.

"Yeah," I said. "Just ten minutes—that'll leave you the whole rest of the day to play cops and robbers, or cowboys and Indians, or whatever the hell it is that you do here."

The Chief sneered, then stretched out his arm. "Have a seat, boys," he said, gesturing at a couple of chairs beside his desk. "The sooner we can get this over with the better."

The Chief waited for Monty and me to sit and then went back behind his desk and planted his butt on his throne. His chair was about half a foot higher than ours, so he was able to look down on us. It was his way of making up for the height discrepancy. He fiddled with one of the toys on his desk—a wind-up cat. Maybach craned his head to get a closer look at it.

"Is that a Norwegian Forest Cat?" Maybach asked.

"You've got a good eye," the Chief said. "This was given to me by the Old Judge himself as a show of appreciation for my work at the 1988 cat show."

"What happened there?" Maybach asked.

"Faulty cages. One of the springs popped and a couple of cats got loose. I found 'em though. And one of them was the eventual winner. A calico just like this one."

The two of them went on about cats for another few minutes, while I remained silent. The Chief clasped his hands pedantically. "But I'm sure you didn't come by to chat about cats," he said. "So tell me, what's on your minds?"

"How come you let your boys trample the crime scene this morning?" I asked right off the bat. I wanted to wipe the smug grin off his face and directness always seemed the best method. "Did you order it, or are they just comically incompetent?"

The Chief leaned forward. He stared me straight in the eye while I watched his face turn two different shades of red. Then he hopped off his highchair and quickly moved to the door to his office, which had been wide open this whole time. He grasped the door knob and pulled the door shut. Then Little Napoleon returned to his throne. Much calmer now, his natural coloring returned.

"I'd appreciate it if you'd keep your voices down," he said. "People are trying to work out there."

"On what?" I asked. "Basket weaving for the crafts fair? Cuz they sure as hell aren't doing any police work."

Before his color turned back to fire engine red, I made a peace offering.

"Tell you what," I said. "You don't have to answer that last question. How about you just prove me wrong, and let us take a look at the case files instead?"

"I'm sure you already know as much as we do," the Chief said coyly. "Big city fellow like you."

"I'd just like to take a look at some of the evidence you collected. Ballistics, blood sampling, tire prints . . . you know, the usual stuff any cadet at the academy would know how to do."

The Chief scrunched up his face. He clasped his hands. He leaned in. "I really don't think it would be wise for you to go poking around in things you don't understand."

"Such as?" I asked.

"Yes," Monty spoke up. "What wouldn't we understand?"

The Chief sighed. Then he shook his head from side to side. He threw his arms up, as if defeated.

"Either of you big shots know how Olde Sayville got its name?"

I looked at Monty, who shrugged. I shook my head.

"Aha," the Chief continued. "Looks like you boys need a little history lesson. The people from the Salem witch hunts founded this place."

"Yes, I knew that," Maybach interrupted.

"But did you know that Sayville is short for Salem Village?" he shot back. "Putting it all together now?"

"So it extrapolates out to Olde Salem Village?" Monty asked.

"Exactly," the Chief said. He gave us a knowing nod and a wink.

"So fucking what?" I said.

The Chief leaned in. "The curse," he whispered. He looked at us as if what he said actually meant something.

"Could you elaborate, please?" Maybach asked after a brief

pause.

"The Hathorne family. First you had William Hathorne back in the early 1600s. He thought it was his duty to persecute Quakers. But his son, the infamous Judge John Hathorne—he took it all to a different level. How much do you actually know about the Salem witch trials of 1692?"

"Twenty people were strung up for being witches," I chimed in.

"Actually," the Chief said, "only nineteen of them were strung up. One was pressed to death for refusing to answer any questions. Here's the thing, though. In 1711—nineteen years after they were executed—all twenty of them were exonerated. And every single one of the judges involved repented for his actions in the trial. All but one, that is."

"Let me take a guess," I said. "Judge John Hathorne?"

"Now you're catching on. Let me tell you something—three hundred years isn't as much water under the bridge as you may think."

"Meaning what exactly?" Maybach asked.

The Chief shook his head and smiled smugly. "Perspective, gentlemen. Some people may call it a curse, whereas others'll call it karma. And some may call it payback. My job isn't to differentiate semantics, though; my job is to determine whether this curse, karma, payback—whatever you want to call it—is premeditated."

"And is it?" I asked.

"We'll just have to wait and see. The important thing is not to open up a Pandora's Box here. Once the curse is let out, you can't get it back in."

"You don't really believe in it, though." I said.

The Chief made a funny face, as if my last question gave him gastric discomfort. "Honestly," he said, "I don't know whether I do or not. I mean, none of us were around when the curse was in high gear. All I know is that people kept on dying until it was somehow exorcised. We had the bejeezuz scared out of us then, and our number one job here is to prevent it from resurfacing. You understand?"

"So your police procedures are to leave well enough alone, then?" Maybach asked.

"You know why those Witch trials happened? Cuz you got a bunch of rich know-nothings—like Hathorne—all of a sudden asked to play investigator. You know what qualified him to be a judge?"

"His wallet?" I asked.

"That's right, Dodge," he answered. "And because he had an agenda, he wouldn't accept any answer other than the one he was looking for. If they all had just looked the other way, the accusers would've grown tired of accusing, and life would've gone on pretty much unaltered. And no one would've gotten hurt."

"Except that now a murder has already been committed—and there's the promise of more to come," Maybach said. "Perhaps you need to employ a different investigative technique?"

"Yeah," I added. "You already tried doing nothing, but that didn't seem to work."

"Don't you worry. We'll find the murderer," he said. "And soon. You can count on that. Just have to give us a little leeway. We've got to give the curse its due."

I thought about the Rangers. Anytime the "curse" was mentioned, it automatically triggered it. The Rangers became cursed after they won the Stanley Cup in 1940. According to legend, the Rangers' owners had made their final mortgage payment on Madison Square Garden, and celebrated by burning the mortgage papers in the Cup. The hockey Gods—not to mention the entire country of Canada—were offended that Lord Stanley's Cup was being desecrated, and a curse was cast upon the Rangers. (There's another variation of the curse as well: The other hockey team in New York at the time, the New York Americans, were forced out of the league, largely due to the muscling of the Rangers ownership. It is said that the former owner of the Americans then cast a similar curse on the Rangers.) Whether one believed in the curse or not, the Rangers still went 54 years without winning another Cup—so I enlisted God to intervene in 1994. One could say that my prayers had far less to do with it than Mark Messier did, but I wasn't going to argue with the result. So when the Chief cited the curse, a part of me wanted to give him a little bit of wiggle room.

The Chief stood up and opened the door. "You're pretty clever fellows," he said. "I don't imagine you'd need some dumb cop to spell it all out for you. Thanks for stopping by, boys." The Chief had his cop/receptionist usher us out of the mom-and-pop precinct. The parasitic jumper in my gut started limbering up.

16.
Maybach: A Matter of Perception

DODGE ASKED ME TO TAKE A DETOUR via a dirt road on the way back to Elizabeth's house. We were absolutely livid over the Chief of Police's behavior. How dare he be so dismissive when people's lives were at stake? Obviously there was something else driving him. Deep down, both Dodge and I knew that there was a rather large can of worms that needed to be unearthed.

"Stop right here," Dodge shouted. I pulled over along the side of the road. Dodge got out and walked off a few paces, between two large shade trees. He gazed down at the dirt and cleared some leaves and branches away. Then he pulled out his camera and snapped about ten pictures of the dirt.

"What was that all about?" I asked him when he returned to the car.

"Just trying to eliminate some suspects," he said. "How about we drop in on Lydia?"

"Unannounced?" I asked.

"I've got a feeling she's expecting me."

"Would you mind if we checked on Dash and Lil first?" I asked. "My hotel is on the way."

Dodge agreed, provided I uncork one of my bottles of wine. As it was fast approaching lunch time, I assented, and planned the menu on the drive over. I grabbed some essentials at a nearby market—I'd whip up a tomato and peach gazpacho, and make skewers of coriander grilled shrimp and charred tomato. It would decently complement the Barossa Valley Shiraz I had back at my hotel. I also picked up some fresh cod for Dash and Lil.

My Persian beauties eagerly greeted me, in stark contrast to their indifference at my departure earlier that morning. And also because they likely smelled the fresh fish I had for them in the grocery bag. Dodge didn't want to eat anything at first, but I insisted. I told him that it was a non-negotiable stipulation if he wished to partake of the Shiraz.

Despite the lack of a formal kitchen in my hotel room, I was able to whip up the meal thanks to my traveling gourmet kit. It was basically a set of interchangeable kitchen utensils that fit into a wooden handle base, and a set of stacking trays and saucepans inside a miniature convection oven. It all fit neatly in its own tote bag, and could be carried over the shoulder. Back when I was just starting out in the food industry, and at the insistence of my dear friend, Geoffrey, I tried to sell my traveling gourmet kit on late-night television. I wanted to call it "Gourmet on the Go," or "Gourmet to Go," but unfortunately, both names were already taken and registered. So I settled on "Gourmet-a-Go-Go"—not only was the name available and unregistered, I thought it very cute and catchy. What I didn't realize, however, was that there was a rather infamous underground sex club for food fetishists by that name. Inside the walls of Gourmet-a-Go-Go (or "the GaGG," as it was often referred to by its patrons), unspeakable acts were performed nightly upon glazed ducks, rump roasts, countless pâtés, and every type of dessert imaginable. Given the fact that my commercials were aired very late at night, and often interspersed among ads for various sex chat hotlines, the assumption was made that I was selling my wares to this targeted clientele. The "Gourmet-a-Go-Go" quickly became the butt of many jokes in the food industry. I immediately pulled the commercials from the airwaves, and set out to clear my name and restore my reputation. Even with the help of Geoffrey, it still took well over a year before I was able to book my next catering job.

"Damn, this is good," Dodge said after interchangeably slurping up the gazpacho and gulping down the Shiraz. "No wonder they keep asking you back."

"I take that as the greatest of compliments, Phil."

Now that I had endeared myself to Dodge's palate, I tried to gain access to his thoughts.

"Don't you think it's about time we both put all our cards on the table? After all, the police have already proven themselves to be less than helpful."

Dodge finished his glass and pointed to the bottle. "May I?" he asked.

"Allow me," I said and refilled his goblet. Dodge took another gulp, as I placed a shrimp kabob on his plate.

"All right, Monty," he said, while eating straight from the skewer. "Tell me everything you know about Chip Danforth."

Chip Danforth? Why would Dodge ask me about Chip Danforth?

"Certainly," I said. "But perhaps first you should tell me what you were taking pictures of on that dirt road."

"Tire treads," he answered simply and without elaboration. He took another nibble of shrimp. "Your turn. What's up with Chip Danforth? How come he threw the golf tournament?"

"Threw? What are you talking about?" I was floored by his allegation.

"Come on, Monty," he said. "I thought you wanted us to put all our cards on the table. Did Eliot Stoughton have something on him?"

"You astound me with your accusations."

"You're still too close to these people, Monty," he said. "You can't see the forest for the trees. Give yourself some distance."

I became incensed. "How dare you?"

"Okay, fine," Dodge said. "Let me walk you through it. Bryce Danforth was murdered. Do you believe that anyone at the club is capable of such an act?"

"Not from my experiences with them," I replied.

"Yet," Dodge added. "You said yourself that the letter writer must be someone from the club, right?"

I began to see Dodge's logic. He was right. I was looking at it through rose-tinted lenses. I was letting my earlier perceptions get in the way of my observations. Obviously, the way I perceived at least one of the club members must be incorrect. I thought for a moment about Chip Danforth and Eliot Stoughton.

"Chip had won the last two tournaments," I said, more thinking out loud than making a statement. "So he would already be used to the pressure, and highly unlikely to double-bogey the last hole. Whereas Eliot has a nervous condition, and would probably only be able to make his final putt if he knew he was assured victory no matter what he did."

"Bravo, Monty," Dodge said clapping his hands. "Bravo."

I thought some more. "But why?" I asked rhetorically.

"Now's when you get to draw on your experiences," Dodge said. "What kind of person is Chip Danforth? Is this something he would do for money, or would he need to be threatened?"

Dodge was good. He knew all the right questions to ask. But his big city experiences also clouded his observations.

"Or perhaps," I said, "he did it out of kindness."

"You're still stuck in the forest, Monty. Take a few more steps back."

"Perhaps you're the one stuck in the urban jungle," I offered. "People are different here."

"Sure they are. That's why they kidnap cats . . . or break their cages so they can escape. That's different, all right."

"Are you referring to the Norwegian Forest Cat incident of 1988?" I asked.

"You don't really believe what the Chief said about faulty cages, right?"

I didn't, in fact. The Norwegian Forest Cat was a relatively new breed, and had just been certified for competition by the Cat Fanciers Association in 1987. I suspected that some traditionalist objected to the new breed's participation and liberated the cat.

"I'm sure that had more to do with pride than malice," I answered. "I assure you, it was more of a breed issue."

"You think a Sphinx can win?" Dodge asked, startling me with his knowledge of cats.

"Have you ever seen a Sphinx?"

"Nope. All I know is that Chip has one, and Blake doesn't think it can win."

"Not just Blake," I answered.

My dear friend, Geoffrey, once described Sphinxes as "cats on chemo." The Sphinx has no fur, just a nearly invisible coat of fuzz, which feels like a swirl of velvet. But from a distance it appears to be a totally bald cat. I explained this to Dodge.

"So, I honestly don't believe a Sphinx has a chance of winning," I said.

"Unless, of course, the competition was eliminated," he said.

"I'm sorry, Phil. Knowing Chip Danforth as I do, I can't believe that he's capable of murder."

Dodge looked as if he was about to lecture me again about being too close—too much of an insider—but then, uncharacteristically, stopped himself. Instead his face drooped, causing the enormous bags beneath his eyes to practically touch his chin. He spoke softly.

"I don't want to believe that Lydia Danforth is capable of murder either." He seemed genuinely sad.

"Nor do I," I said.

Dodge rubbed his stomach, then finished his entire glass of wine in one giant gulp.

"But," Dodge continued, "I can't let my personal feelings get in the way of the numbers." He dropped his head, as if defeated. "Forget about Chip and Eliot for now," he said, then took a deep breath. "Let's get over to Lydia's house."

17.
Dodge: The Lady Vanishes

LYDIA WASN'T HOME. Even though she begged me to come visit her. Not home. So Maybach and I headed back to Elizabeth's house. But when we arrived, the place was crawling with cops. The glow of the sirens greeted us as we made our ascent up the hill. I had a horrible feeling. And it wasn't just because my abdominal athlete was doing heavy calisthenics—a sense of dread overtook me. It seemed like an eternity before Maybach pulled into the driveway. I couldn't wait any longer. I jumped out of the car while it was still moving, and sprinted into the house.

When I reached the parlor, a body covered with a blood-stained sheet was lying in the middle of the room; the newly replaced glass in the bay window had been shattered once again, but this time the projectile had reached its mark. The mini-Olympian proceeded to kick every organ in my body, and came down especially hard on my heart. I'd left Elizabeth alone. I was supposed to protect her. Just like Valerine Rizzo—only this time I should have known better. I looked down again at the body. I flashed back to the day at the morgue when they pulled the sheet off Valerine's corpse. Twenty-six stab wounds. I hadn't been very subtle in trying to track down her ex-husband, and didn't do much to cover my tracks. He found out that some guy named Phil Dodge was looking for him, so he hired his own P.I. to follow me. The P.I. provided him with photos of Valerine and me in bed.

He hunted her down, kidnapped her, tortured her, and then stabbed her to death. Afterwards, the bastard calmly climbed out his window onto his fire escape, then dove off and took a header into the pavement. And as it turned out, the jewels had been sold off months earlier. Valerine could've just walked into a pawn shop and bought them. Only I never bothered to find out that information. I was too busy screwing her.

"Looks like you missed quite a bit of excitement," a familiar voice said, pulling me back into the present situation. I turned around and saw the Napoleonic Chief of Police walking toward me.

"Can I see her?" I asked, my voice tinged with desperation.

"*Her?* Well, now how would you know whether that's a man or a woman under there?" he asked accusingly.

"Let me see her," I snarled. The Chief backed off.

"It's a good thing for you that you happened to be sitting in my office at the time of the shooting," he said. Then the Chief looked over to one of his men and nodded. The cop dutifully pulled the sheet from the body.

"Good lord," I heard a gasping Maybach shriek behind me. "Poor dear Wanda!"

I looked down at Wanda's corpse. A gray mop of hair covered half of her colorless face. The cop pushed away the hair to reveal a bullet hole through her forehead. The blood had already begun to dry and crust up, leaving a darkened black outline around the wound. I felt a lump form in the back of my throat. I was relieved that it wasn't Elizabeth under the sheet, but felt guilty that it came at Wanda's expense. I looked back to the Chief.

"Elizabeth?" I managed to ask, while keeping the lump at bay.

"She's upstairs under a heap of blankets," the Chief said. "Shivering. That bullet was meant for her."

★ ★ ★

I HELD HER CLOSE AGAINST ME. A trembling hodgepodge of beauty, hysteria, fear, denial and regret.

"This can't be happening, Phil. Not Wanda! And it's all my fault. It was me they were after."

She pressed her lips on my ear, and whispered, "Promise me you'll never leave me again."

"Sure thing," I whispered back. I squeezed her tight. For a brief moment, I imagined she was Valerine. I lost control of myself—I kissed her long and hard on the mouth. And she kissed me back. Out of fear, perhaps. Then she quickly pulled away from the embrace; stunned by her actions. "Forgive me," she said. "I'm not myself."

"It's not your fault," I said. "I never should have left you alone in the first place."

She put her arms around me. She was still shaking. "Make me warm, Phil." She pulled herself closer to me, and I held her tight. I felt her shivers now, as she quaked against me. She wrapped her left leg around my right leg. And then I kissed her again. With passion. Her shivers subsided.

"Thank you, Phil," she sighed. "You're most kind for indulging me."

She kissed me one more time, and then began to straighten out her clothes. It was as if she had just remembered that she was a lady in high society. "We'd best go downstairs," she said. "I'm sure the police have more questions for me."

"Yes," I agreed. As I escorted Elizabeth down the grand staircase, I relived the last few minutes; drinking in her wonderful smell and remembering the taste of her lips. Then I thought about God. He and I appeared to be moving closer to being back on speaking terms. Monty interrupted my spiritual thoughts before we reached the landing.

"I'm going to the hotel to fetch my things," he said. "The Chief and I have been discussing the situation, and we both think it would be best if I moved in here for the time being. It will be extra security for Elizabeth."

"Why not station an armed cop here, then?" I asked. "Wouldn't that make more sense?"

"I doubt you'll be able to find one with my culinary skills," Maybach said. "I'll be taking over the cooking."

"That's wonderful, Monty," Elizabeth said before I could register my protest. "You are always welcome here."

I handed Elizabeth off to the Chief of Police for questioning. "Over your shivers, Mrs. Hathorne?" the Chief asked with a little too much attitude in his voice for my comfort. I gave Elizabeth a reassuring pat on the shoulder.

"You don't mind if we ask you to wait outside, Mr. Dodge, do you?" the Chief asked. "After all, that's textbook police procedure, now isn't it? We're gonna need to question you a little later on. See if your story corroborates or not."

"S.O.P. is to keep the suspects separated BEFORE you question them, Chief."

"That's okay," he said. "Didn't seem to me like you two were doing a whole lot of talking up there anyway."

The smug bastard shut the door on my face. But it was a needed reality check. I had to focus on the case again. I wondered where Lydia Danforth was, and what she'd been up to. I ran outside to see if I could catch Monty before he left. He had his face in the trunk of the Mercedes, chewing on one of his chocolate helpers. They had begun to melt from the heat and I could see a trail of chocolate across Maybach's face, leading down to his chin.

"I promised Elizabeth I wouldn't leave again," I said. "See if you can track down Lydia, and find out where the hell she's been. Swing by her house first, then check the club."

"Really?" he said with mock surprise. "I never would have thought of that on my own. Maybe it was just pure dumb luck that I called Lloyd's house a few minutes ago and found it rather curious that Lydia answered the phone. I was planning on taking a ride over there right now, but if you think I should go to the club instead . . ." He popped another chocolate in his mouth.

"Well, what the hell are you doing wasting time talking to me then?" I said awkwardly, trying to save face.

"You must have read my mind," he said. He wiped his chocolate-stained hands and chin with his oversized handkerchief, until it looked like a freshly soiled, monogrammed diaper. Then he closed the trunk, wobbled into the driver's seat and sped off. And he didn't even offer me one of his chocolates.

18.
Maybach: Tennis Anyone?

LLOYD PROCTOR LIVED ON THE OUTSKIRTS of Olde Sayville, on the other side of the tracks, in both the literal and figurative sense of the phrase. Although there were no impoverished parts of Olde Sayville, he lived in the more modest, non-filthy rich neighborhood. He was the resident tennis pro at the Olde Sayville Society. And while he was merely an employee, he had managed to work his way into the graces of many of the members. He was very slick. Perhaps a little too slick for his own good. I knew that he had engaged in affairs with many of the female club members, but I had never suspected Lydia as being one of his conquests. Even though it was common knowledge that he was defiling a good many of the membership's female contingency, his job there was secure—he was especially adept at prying secrets from these women. Any suggestion of his termination would precipitate the release of these tidbits of forbidden knowledge.

I pulled into the driveway of Lloyd's bungalow-style house, and parked beside Lydia's Lexus. Lloyd's car was conspicuously absent.

"Hello, Monty," Lydia said greeting me at the front door. "What brings you all the way out here?"

"I might very well ask you the same question," I answered.

"I couldn't stand being in that house any more. Everything around me reminded me of Bryce and the murder. I just needed to take my mind off of it."

"I see. Where's Lloyd?"

"I don't know," she said. "I tried calling but there was no answer, so I decided I'd just wait for him. I know where he keeps his spare key hidden."

That was a bit of news I wasn't prepared to hear. Perhaps I'd overestimated Lydia's virtue, and she *was* one of Lloyd's conquests—which would give both of them more of a motive for Bryce's murder.

Lydia invited me in, and I immediately took inventory of Lloyd's kitchen, and the contents of his refrigerator. I needed to pry information from Lydia, and creating some culinary masterpiece seemed the best way to loosen her lips—after all, I was well aware that she had a weakness for frittatas, and Lloyd had plenty of eggs and fresh vegetables available. But it seemed that my recent encounters with Phil Dodge had altered my typical protocol, and rather than looking for a skillet, I found myself taking a more direct approach.

"Are you and Lloyd having an affair?" I asked. Even I was shocked by the directness and rudeness of the inquiry.

"What's gotten into you, Monty?" she said, taken aback.

"A little bit of Phil Dodge, I'm afraid."

"Did he put you up to this? Is he jealous or something?"

I froze. I pretended not to be surprised by her last comment. Instead, I chose to roll with it.

"Well, Lydia, you must understand," I said to buy myself a few more seconds to think how to proceed; then "'Jealous' is a rather strong word," I offered up. "But what can you expect really?" I had no idea what I was talking about.

"Boy," she said. "I never would've figured him to be the kind to kiss and tell."

Clarity. Horrible clarity. I was speechless.

"Do you think less of me now, Monty?" she asked. "Do you think I'm a whore? It was okay for Bryce to go gallivanting behind my back with Elizabeth all this time, but not for me to have an indiscretion?"

"Elizabeth and Bryce?" I exclaimed. "Impossible!"

"That's what I thought at first, too," she said.

"How do you know this for sure?" I asked.

"Lloyd told me all about it six months ago. He told me they'd been meeting secretly; but just like you, I didn't believe him. So he showed me pictures."

"Pictures? Of what?"

"The two of them checking into a motel in New Hampshire. Checking out as well," she tried to suppress a whimper.

"Lloyd took these pictures, I suppose?"

"Yes."

Of course he did. Just another way for Lloyd to insure that his contract with the Olde Sayville Society was extended. There was nothing the least bit shocking about it.

"And is that why you're here right now?" I asked.

The crying began. "Yes," she sobbed. "I don't want these getting out and blemishing Bryce's memory. And I'm trying to persuade Lloyd to give them to me. I'm not evil, Monty. I'm just trying to be a good wife."

Not even the most succulent of my blue ribbon roasts could have yielded this sort of information. I made a mental note to overhaul my modus operandi in the future.

"Do you think he'll give them to you?" I asked.

"He has to," she answered boldly, wiping away her tears. "There's absolutely nothing that I won't do to get them."

I heard sirens outside. The police were paying a visit. I was running out of time and I wanted to question Lydia before the police did.

"Lydia, do you know anything about the shooting that took place at the Hathorne estate earlier today?"

Her eyes lit up a little, but before she had a chance to answer my question, the twelve-year-old policeman came inside with two other pre-pubescent officers flanking him.

"Lydia Danforth?" he asked.

"Yes," she replied.

"Ma'am," he said. "I'm sorry to inform you that I have a warrant for your arrest."

"What's the charge?" I demanded, inserting myself into the fray.

"The murders of Bryce Danforth and Wanda Williams," he said.

"Wanda?" she asked incredulously. "It was Wanda?"

"And the attempted murder of Elizabeth Hathorne," the cop added.

She let loose with a desperate howl as the cop read Lydia her rights and placed her in handcuffs.

"Monty," Lydia called to me between bawling yowls, while the police removed her from the premises. "You know I didn't do it, right?"

"Of course, my dear," I said to her. But I wasn't at all certain.

19.
Dodge: Chills and Thrills

AS THE CHIEF WAS WRAPPING UP OUR INTERVIEW, he alerted me that an arrest was forthcoming.

"Arresting a witch or something?" I asked him.

He screwed up his face and looked at me like I was nuts.

"I mean, I guess it would have to be some sort of a witch who was responsible for this Olde Salem Village curse, right?" I clarified. The Chief gave me a broad smile and chuckled softly. He patted me on the back and then leaned in.

"You'll keep your nose out of this, Dodge, if you have any sense of self-preservation," he said softly, while still grinning widely. "You're out of your element." Then the Chief had his boys cart off Wanda's body and disappeared from the Hathorne estate.

Elizabeth had the chills again. I asked her if she had these often, but she said it was something new she'd been experiencing for the last week or so. Right around the time the first poisoned pen letter arrived.

"I suppose you must think I'm psychosomatic," she said, half-joking. "Sometimes I think it myself."

I told her she was in good company, and explained about my bleeding ulcer and the accompanying Olympic games that were being conducted on my busted up organs. She laughed until she felt another shiver and grabbed a hold of me, as if she were clutching for dear life.

"What's the matter?" I asked.

"You're going to think I'm crazy," she said.

"You'll be in good company," I said. "Try me."

"Well, it's just that my late husband would often tremble, and he complained about being very cold only a few weeks before he died." She snuggled up against my chest for warmth. "It just seems too much like a coincidence, what with all this talk of the curse."

I put an arm around her and stroked her back gently. "But your husband was eighty-one years old, right?" I said trying to put her mind at ease. "Trembling and cold aren't all that uncommon at that age."

"I suppose," she said, unconvinced. I held her for a few moments until enough time had passed such that it was appropriate to question her some more about the case.

"So what did you end up telling the police?"

"Why, the truth, of course," she said, pushing away defensively. Apparently not enough time had passed yet for me to pursue this line of questioning.

"Of course," I said, pulling her back into my chest. "It's just that I don't know any of the details about how Wanda was killed, and the cops are keeping me in the dark about it. I was just wondering if you could tell me what you told them."

"Sorry," she said. "I'm a little on edge." She drew a deep breath and recounted the story. "Despite taking that pill, I was unable to fall asleep. I was just so cold. I didn't want to risk taking another one, so I came downstairs and asked Wanda to get some of the winter blankets out of storage."

"Where were you?"

"I was standing in the parlor, not far from the window. At the time Wanda was leaning over, polishing the coffee tables. She quickly stood up and took a step toward the cedar closet where the blankets are stored. But as soon as she stepped between me and the window, the glass shattered, and Wanda fell down. Dead." She closed her eyes, as if reliving it. Tears began to stream down.

"Did they ask you anything else?" I said, while brushing the tears away from her cheek.

"Like what?" she asked.

"Just typical cop questions," I said. "Like why you didn't use the intercom, or why you didn't get the blankets yourself?"

"No," she said harshly, and pushed me away. "They didn't ask me anything like that. Apparently my word is good enough for them."

"It's good enough for me too," I said calmly, trying not to back down. I had to get through this line of questioning.

"I happened to have tried the intercom," she said defensively, "but Wanda didn't answer. So I came downstairs to get the blankets out of the closet myself, but when Wanda saw me, she insisted that she do it."

"Do you mind if I take a look in the cedar closet?" I asked.

"I've got nothing to hide," she said.

She was angry at me. Maybe it was for the best—if there were less sexual tension, maybe I could better focus on the case. I opened the closet and poked around. The winter blankets were stored in an ornate trunk that looked like an antique. It had elaborate etchings on each of the panels, depicting scenes from English history, beginning with the Battle of Hastings in one corner, and ending with the post-Cromwell Restoration. There was so much detail, I learned more from this trunk than I did from any history class I ever took. (Although, it's quite likely that I was cutting school to play broom hockey when the subject was being taught.) It struck me as odd that such a stunning—and obviously expensive—piece of furniture like this was hidden away in the closet. I removed the blankets and handed them to Elizabeth. Something didn't seem right, though. Spatially. The trunk looked bigger on the outside than on the inside. I ran my hand along the inside, tapping my fingers as I went. Then I heard a hollow thud. The fake siding came off with a twist and a pull, revealing a secret compartment. Inside the compartment were three unlabeled jars filled with reddish-brown powder, which I gently removed.

"What on earth . . . ?" Elizabeth asked.

I unscrewed the cap on one of the jars and took a quick whiff. Strong and medicinal, with a hint of a licorice smell. I quickly screwed the cap back on. Suddenly it was all starting to make sense.

"When Wanda saw you going into the closet, how did she behave?" I asked.

"I already told you; she insisted that she get the blankets."

"But did she seem frazzled at all?"

"Well, now that you mention it, she did seem sort of on edge. I suppose I thought it peculiar at the moment, but then the shot rang out, and it never really registered with me."

The fog in my mind started to clear. I could see now why Wanda didn't want Elizabeth going anywhere near the blankets.

"Your husband didn't die of natural causes," I said. "He was poisoned. And I've got a feeling that you've been poisoned, too."

She looked at me stunned. "You don't mean to say . . ."

"I do," I said cutting her off. "Wanda poisoned your husband, and she's been poisoning you, too."

She thought long and hard.

"I suppose it's possible," she finally said. "She certainly had control over everything we ate. But why?"

"Maybe she was in love with your husband," I said. "Who knows what the circumstances were. Before he met you, there were a good fifteen years when she was the only woman in his life, right? For all we know they could have been having an affair then."

"I seriously doubt that," she said proudly. "You never met my husband."

"Nonetheless," I continued, not wishing to get into an argument over this point, "whether it was reciprocated or not, she was in love with him," I said. I thought back to Wanda's attempt to strangle me with the bowtie at the very hint of my criticizing the Judge.

"But if she was in love with him, why would she kill him?" Elizabeth asked.

"Maybe because she couldn't have him. Love can make you do some pretty hateful things." I thought again about Valerine Rizzo. Her husband never wanted the divorce. The only reason he took the jewels was because he knew they had sentimental value to Valerine and that she'd likely try to retrieve them. That was his plan: he'd get to see her again when she came looking for the jewels. But she hired me to find them instead—which I never got around to doing. So when no one came inquiring about the jewels, he got desperate and pawned them. And when he discovered that some guy named Dodge was sleeping with his ex-wife, he couldn't take it anymore. The old "if I can't have you nobody can" routine. At least that's what it said in the police report.

"The person who shot Wanda," Elizabeth said, jolting me back into reality. "Did they do it to protect me, or were they actually trying to kill me and missed?"

"That's just one of the questions I've got," I answered. "Let's suppose Wanda's killer was really aiming for you. Were they in cahoots with Wanda, or were they working separately? Was Wanda the letter writer? Or did the letter writer kill Wanda?"

"All good questions," she said.

"But now suppose this person was actually aiming for Wanda. Were they trying to protect you from Wanda, and if so, how would they know that she was poisoning you? How many people are involved? Exactly how big is this thing?" I thought about the Chief's history lesson. How far-reaching was this so-called curse/karma/payback?

"You'll make everything right again, won't you?" she said, nuzzling me. "I just know you will." Her very touch caused my mind to fog up again. She was just so damn irresistible. Was this God's doing? Had He found yet another way to spite and torture me?

"We should get you to a hospital," I said.

"No, I'm fine. Really," she said. "I just want you to hold me. That's the only medicine I want right now."

"I can hold you at the hospital, too," I said.

"But you can't do this at the hospital," she said and planted a long wet kiss on my lips.

"Or this," she continued, this time fondling my buttocks while nibbling on my ear. "I'm feeling warmer already. I think you're the antidote I need." She placed her gloved finger on my belt buckle. I was caught somewhat off-guard by her sexual aggressiveness. It was a side of Elizabeth that I hadn't seen; but I certainly wasn't going to complain about it.

"Let's go up to my boudoir," she said. "I'd hate for Monty to walk in on us right now."

"Not nearly as much as I would," I said, lifting her into my arms. I carried Elizabeth up the stairs and into her bedroom. Through this improbable sequence of events, I was about to see how the other half lived. She undressed me first, and told me to get into the bed and lie under the covers. I complied immediately. Then she did a slow, seductive and uninhibited striptease. Soon she was dancing topless for me, wearing nothing but a pair of white lace panties and her elbow-length gloves.

"What would you like me to take off next?" she asked playfully. I flashed back to my dinner-time fantasy about her wearing nothing but the gloves. A moment later it became a reality. She removed her panties, lifted the covers and crept toward me.

And she began to outdo her shadow. God and I were back on speaking terms.

20.
Maybach: A Conflict of Interest

WE CHECKED OUT OF THE HOTEL, much to Dash and Lil's chagrin. They had finally gotten acclimated to the suite and hissed at me when I put them into their carrying case. We were now on our way to Elizabeth's house. I wondered if Dodge had heard the news about Lydia's arrest yet. And if he hadn't I wanted to break the news to him gently. After all, Dodge had been intimate with her, and likely harbored some very strong feelings. But I couldn't allow his feelings to get in the way of our investigation.

When I arrived at Elizabeth's house, I had to wait quite a while before Dodge finally answered the door and let me in. He seemed rather perturbed by my arrival. Perhaps he was still feeling uncomfortable about me working on the case with him. I was certain that his attitude would change after I told him about the information I'd gathered.

"Where's Elizabeth?" I asked.

"Upstairs," he said.

"What took you so long to answer the door?"

"That was Wanda's job," he said.

"Poor dear Wanda," I said.

"Did you manage to track down Lydia?" Dodge asked gruffly.

I took a deep breath. I placed my hand on Dodge's wrist, and looked him right in the eye. It was time to break the news to him.

"Phil," I said, "I'm afraid that Lydia's been arrested."

"What?"

"For the murders of Bryce and Wanda, and for the attempted murder of Elizabeth." I gave him all the information as quickly as possible.

"Based on what evidence?" Dodge asked testily.

"Now calm down," I said.

"I *am* calm," he shouted, belying his statement as he delivered it.

"Phil," I said, trying to be both a friend and a co-investigator. "I know all about it. You're just letting your personal feelings get in the way."

"Don't be a sap," he said dismissively. But I refused to be dismissed. I pressed the issue.

"I know that this news must be very hard on you," I said. "I know that you and Lydia have been intimate together."

"What?!" I heard a voice cry out. It was Elizabeth. She had just made it down the steps. She was dressed rather strangely, wearing a lounging robe and a pair of gloves.

"You and Lydia?" she accused Dodge like a jealous lover. "How could you?"

"Elizabeth," Dodge said, turning toward her and trying to grab her hand.

"Don't you touch me," she said. "In fact, why don't you pack up and go."

Dodge tried to speak, but Elizabeth immediately cut him off. "Your services are no longer required, Mr. Dodge. I didn't even hire you in the first place. Bryce did. Why don't you go collect your money from Lydia and get the hell out of Olde Sayville." She began to storm off, but then turned back. She still had more to say. "And you can take Lydia Danforth with you for all I care." Then she ran toward the steps, but Dodge ran faster and intercepted her.

"Let me explain," he said. Elizabeth slapped him across the face. And it was quite a wallop. Even though she was wearing gloves, it still left a mark. She looked at her hand and then back to Dodge.

"Mr. Dodge," she said, composing herself, "You are no longer welcome in this house. If you don't leave the premises immediately, I will call the police and have you arrested for trespassing." Then she pushed past him and continued upstairs. Before she made it to the landing, her icy exterior had melted, and given way to poorly muffled sobs. She ran into a room and slammed the door shut. Dodge turned and walked toward me. He had a dangerous look in his eye.

"Give me your fucking car keys," he said.

"Not in front of the cats," I gently reminded him.

"Give me your fucking car keys!" he shouted. And he made extra sure to pronounce the f-word as loudly and clearly as he could. Apparently this was not the time to work on his vocabulary. Under the circumstances, I quickly handed him my car keys.

"Where are you going?" I asked.

"You heard the lady," he said. "I'm gonna get my money and get the hell out of this town."

"But the investigation . . ."

"It's all yours, Monty. Because if I stay here another minute, the cops'll have another corpse on their hands—and you'll be in no position to help out from the morgue."

I stayed out of Dodge's way as he gathered his few belongings, all of which fit into the pockets of his light overcoat. He walked past me on his way to the door.

"My train leaves at four-thirty. You can pick up your car at the train station any time after that. I'll leave your keys in the glove compartment," he said. He looked at me with his sad brown eyes. "Take good care of her, Maybach. Don't let anything bad happen to her."

And then he walked out. I heard my car's tires screech a moment later.

I let Dash and Lil out of their carrier. They appeared more at home here in the mansion than at the hotel, and quickly found their way to the kitchen. I followed them in and cooked up some of the leftover cod, and hand-fed it to them. It reminded me of the days when I was first starting out as a chef—long before I had Geoffrey to advise me on my recipes. I would hand-feed my creations (unseasoned, of course) to several extra-finicky cats. If it passed muster with them, then I knew I was on the right track. Dash and Lil seemed to believe I was on the right track with the cod, but then again, neither of them was what one would call finicky. Opinionated, yes; but finicky, no. As they devoured the fish, I found myself ruing Dodge's sudden departure. Strangely, I had actually grown fond of him.

"I guess it's up to the three of us, now," I said to Dashiell and Lillian. Dash stopped eating momentarily and looked up at me incredulously, as if to say "we're better off without him." Then he stuck his face back into the cod.

21.
Dodge: A Changing of the Guard

I DROVE TO THE CLUB to see if I could collect my money there. When I was hired it wasn't by Bryce, the individual; I was hired by Bryce, the director of the Olde Sayville Society. If my contract were truly terminated, it would need to be done by the Society, not by Elizabeth. When I got to Bryce's former office, there was a new inhabitant moving in. Rudolf was carrying in a cardboard box filled with papers and what looked like someone's personal effects.

"Who's moving in?" I asked.

Rudolf didn't answer. He just put the box down on the desk and headed for the door. I stepped in front of him.

"Didn't your mother ever teach you that it's not polite to ignore people?"

"No, sir, Mr. Dodge," he answered. "I was raised in an orphanage." He paused long enough for me to remove my foot from my mouth before he continued.

"Anyway, I'm not ignoring you, sir," he said. "I'm just not supposed to tell anyone."

"Why not?"

"Loose lips sink ships," he said with a sly wink, and sidestepped his way around me. I decided to have a seat and wait for the Colonel to arrive. Interesting that he was the next in line. One would have thought that due to his seniority, the Colonel would have been ahead of Bryce for the directorship. Yet another piece needing to be fitted into this incongruous puzzle. While I waited, I thought about Elizabeth. She was amazing. I was still reeling from our encounter. And angered by the suddenness with which our all-too-brief affair ended. If only Maybach hadn't interrupted us in the middle, and then opened that fat mouth of his. I pounded my leg with my fist. It wasn't Maybach's fault. Elizabeth would have found out eventually. Lydia wasn't planning on keeping our tryst secret. And she'd likely be recounting the story to the cops and to her lawyer—it was all part of her timeline.

I looked at the portrait of the Judge—we had something in common, now. I stood up and walked around the room. The Judge's eyes followed me wherever I went. Perhaps he could sense that I'd just violated his wife. Or maybe he just knew how much I was in need of a drink. I wondered if anyone knew the combination to the wall safe, behind which resided the smoothest Scotch on the planet—although, at this point, the cheapest rotgut would've done the trick. I pushed the Judge's portrait aside and fingered the dial on the safe. It wasn't much of a lock—I knew third-rate yeggs in the city that could crack it in less than a minute. An old-timer named Benny the Fist once showed me how to trip the tumblers by boring holes in and around the lock. Benny was the least subtle of the safecrackers I knew; a result of his reduced dexterity due to his short stubby fingers. And that's how he got his nickname—even with an open palm, it looked like his hand was balled up in a fist. But his profession made him paranoid, and he locked and bolted his own apartment to such an extreme that Fort Knox could feel comfortable leaving its gold supply under Benny's mattress. Benny felt heart palpitations one night. He called 911 just before he passed out. The emergency vehicles arrived less than two minutes later, but it took them over an hour to break down his door. I still remember the funeral. Closed casket—double-locked, with a latch that could only be tripped from the inside.

"What the hell are you doing?" I heard the Colonel say behind me. I turned around casually and greeted him. Rudolf was standing beside him.

"Congratulations on your new digs," I said.

"Thank you," the Colonel answered humorlessly. "Would you mind moving the portrait back into place?"

"I thought maybe we could celebrate your promotion," I said. "There are some very nice refreshments in there."

The Colonel walked slowly to desk and sat down behind it. Then he looked me straight in the eye.

"What are you doing here, Mr. Dodge?" he asked. He was much more lucid than the first time we'd met. In fact, he seemed to be in full control of his faculties.

"Bryce Danforth hired me on behalf of the Olde Sayville Society. Now that he's gone, I wanted to find out if the new director is still interested in my services."

"Please refresh my memory. Exactly what was it that you were hired to do? I hope to God it wasn't to protect the director from foul play." Not only was he more lucid, he was a lot more cantankerous.

"No. I was hired to protect Elizabeth Hathorne. And currently she's still in one piece. Although another attempt was made on her earlier today."

The Colonel's eyes widened. I expected him to speak, but he remained silent, and just stared at me.

"So my question to you," I said, filling the gaps "is do you want to pay me off now and send me home, or do you want me to continue with the job?"

He scrunched up his face, making his bushy Mark Twain eyebrows look like a white lab rat lounging on the bridge of his nose. He hummed and gurgled, and tapped his fingers against the side of his head, as if he were revving up his brain to process the information. He went on with this humming and tapping routine for about thirty seconds or so. His mental apparatus appeared to be in need of a tune up. I looked over to Rudolf—he just shook his head and smiled.

"Who would protect her if you left now?" the Colonel finally asked.

"Haven't you heard?" I asked. "The police made an arrest."

"Really?" he asked. "Well, that would be a first. Who'd they pinch?" He must have noticed the look of surprise on my face. "Pinch?" he continued. "That is the correct terminology, Mr. Dodge, yes?"

"Yes, it is," I said, trying to stifle a chuckle. "They pinched Lydia Danforth."

The Colonel gasped. He coughed. He gestured to Rudolf, and motioned toward the door. Rudolf obediently exited the office and closed the door behind him on his way out. Apparently, it was time for a private chat. When the Colonel's coughing subsided, he looked me squarely in the eye and asked skeptically, "They think that Lydia killed Bryce?"

"Not just Bryce," I said, "they think she also killed Wanda."

The Colonel began to hyperventilate. His eyes bugged out of his head. He grasped at his heart. Then his face hit the desk.

* * *

AT THE CHIEF'S REQUEST, I paid a little visit to the precinct. After my brief-yet-powerful conversation with the Colonel, Chief Napoleon was insistent that I leave town A.S.A.P., but one of my conditions was seeing Lydia before I left. He agreed, but he wanted to talk to me in his office first. The Chief led me inside and shut the door. He walked around his desk and perched himself upon his throne. "Have a seat, Dodge."

"No thanks," I said. "I don't intend on staying that long." The Chief got flustered. My refusal to sit was undermining his seated height advantage. He stood, walked around the desk and looked me right in the chin.

"You'd best be on the next goddamned train out of town."

"Taking the lord's name in vain?" I cautioned. "In Olde Salem Village? I don't think the founders would approve."

The Chief just smiled. "Think you know it all, don't you?"

"I know you're covering up something."

"You're damn right I am," he said, getting angry. "I have to look the other way all the time. You got no idea the sort of delicate balance I'm dealing with."

Then I got angry. "You small-town, low-life piece of shit. You're trying to pin a double-homicide on an innocent woman to maintain your fucking balance?"

"If anything about this case is certain, it's that Lydia Danforth wrote those letters, killed Wanda and killed her husband."

"How can you be so sure?" I asked.

"Motive. Opportunity. Evidence."

"Evidence?" I challenged. "Like what?"

"Ballistics. We found the gun. She dropped it a couple of yards from the window. We ran a check. It was registered to Lydia Danforth. The slug we picked out of Wanda and the one we pulled out of that sofa matched. Both bullets were fired from that gun."

I thought for a minute. I couldn't be sure if he was lying or not.

"Why didn't she use the gun on Bryce, then?" I asked.

"Crime of passion," he said. "She faked her own cat's disappearance to lure Bryce to the club early. I don't know what her original plan was, but something must've gone wrong, and she ended up bashing his brains in."

I shook my head. "Doesn't add up, Chief," I said. "Suppose the person who stole the cat also stole her gun? Then he could have used it for the shootings."

The Chief smiled, and wagged his finger at me. "Your timeline's off, Mr. Big City Detective. The bullet was shot into the sofa before the cat was snatched." He paused so he could emit a shit-eating grin. "I know she's the one," he said. "Besides, all the crime statistics point to the spouse—numbers don't lie, Dodge."

"Those numbers also include jealous and jilted lovers. You can't apply your stats so selectively," I shot back.

"Okay, bright boy," he continued. "Who's the jealous and/or jilted lover that had access to Lydia's gun, then?" He smirked because he knew I didn't have an answer for it. Maybe I was denying the numbers because I didn't want to believe that Lydia was the one. Still, I persisted.

"She says she has a witness that can testify to her whereabouts when the cat went missing," I said. "Haven't you interviewed Lloyd Proctor?"

"Hasn't been seen since yesterday," the Chief said. "Doesn't matter a lick what that man says. I wouldn't believe him either way."

"And you don't think it's odd that you can't find him?"

"He can't vouch for her when either of the murders occurred, can he? Or during the first murder attempt, right? Who cares about when the cat went missing? Not important."

"How can you say that?" I said. "There was another threatening note left—just like the first one. If you think Lydia wrote those letters, then she must have had something to do with the catnapping, right?"

"Could have been a copycat," he said.

"In that case, your investigation is still open, isn't it?"

"She's the one," the Chief said adamantly. "Lydia killed her husband, and she wanted to kill Elizabeth, too. Still does. She insists Elizabeth and Bryce were having an affair—there's your motive for both killings. Case closed. Unless, of course, you want to explore that jealous-jilted lover angle. But as I recall, you were standing right next to Elizabeth when that bullet came through the window, isn't that right?"

I didn't answer.

"You ever hear of Occam's Razor, Dodge? Let's not make this any more complicated than it is." He cleared the toys off his desk and then made the grand gesture of slamming a stack of papers down. "Here, you can read it in her statement, if you like."

On the surface, Lydia was as guilty as they come. But I still wanted to exhaust every avenue of investigation before I concurred with the Chief.

"I'll ask her myself," I said defiantly. "I don't trust your paperwork. How do I know you didn't fake the ballistics report, too? You already admitted that you cover up all the time. Do you really expect me to believe you?" I was reaching, but I didn't care. Besides, pissing off the Chief was becoming a hobby. The Chief simmered in his chair.

"Well," he finally said. "Either I'm telling you the truth, and she really is a killer; or I'm lying, which means that there's a big conspiracy in this town—one that goes all the way up to the Chief of Police—just to get this woman." He paused and clasped his hands together.

"If Lydia's convicted of Bryce's murder, his last will and testament would probably be contested, wouldn't it?" I asked

"I'd certainly hope so," he said.

"If she can't collect the inheritance, who's next in line?"

The Chief thought for a moment, or at least he pretended to. "Well, they don't have any kids, so I'd guess that would be Bryce's nephew, Chip," he said.

"Perhaps you should be looking into his whereabouts, then?"

"You didn't let me finish, Dodge. I said I'd 'guess' it would be Chip. But it's not. I checked it out. Bryce changed his will last year. Lydia gets the house and cars and an allowance to maintain everything. The rest goes to cancer research. Chip was cut out of it completely."

"Cancer research?" I asked.

"Bryce's mother died from cancer. Very young. Right around the time the Judge lost his second wife to it. That was back in the days when the curse was in full swing."

"What else happened?"

"Well, that was before my time. These are just stories that I heard. But within a two-week period, the Judge's second wife, Bryce's mother, and the Colonel's father all died."

"Let me guess—the Colonel's father had cancer too?"

"No. Freak boating accident. The curse—it works in mysterious ways, I tell you."

The Chief led me out of his office and took me to the jail cells—it looked like a scene out of Andy Griffith, but of course, in a dry town, there was no drunk tank. Just a forlorn woman sitting hopelessly with her head hanging down. Poor Lydia.

"Got a visitor, Mrs. Danforth," the Chief announced, startling her. Her eyes practically leapt out of her head when she saw me. She grabbed me through the prison bars and kissed me hard on the mouth. The bars pushed into my sternum as she pulled me as close to her as she could.

"You've come to help me?"

"If I can," I said. "But I only have a few minutes and I need you to answer some questions. Was your gun really found at the scene, or are the cops just trying to frame you?"

"Frame me, of course," she answered brusquely. "I keep the gun locked in the glove compartment. They probably found it when they searched the car, and then planted it near the house. You have no idea how corrupt this police force is."

"So who do you think did it?" I asked.

"I wish I knew," she said. "Maybe it was Elizabeth," she said dreamily, as if saying it aloud enough times would make it true.

"That would be a pretty good trick," I answered, perhaps a little too quickly. Lydia lashed out.

"Why? Is she fucking you now, too?"

"Calm down," I said, ignoring her last question. "I'm just being logical. First of all, what's her motive? Why would she want to kill Bryce?"

"Lover's spat, maybe."

"Sounds more like a motive for you than for her," I shot back. "But let's say you're right," I continued to appease her. "If it's a lover's spat, why would it take place at the club? And at that hour? And with that weapon? Just doesn't add up, Lydia."

Lydia just laughed. I began to seriously question her mental stability.

"What's so funny?" I asked cautiously, sort of smiling along with her.

"Using the Judge as a weapon," she snickered. "Serves Bryce right."

"How so?"

"Bryce spent a fortune having that damn bust made—just another opportunity to kiss the Judge's ass. That's what catapulted him past the Colonel to second in command there."

So that's how it happened. Bryce pulled a fast one and brown-nosed his way to the top. And considering the Colonel's advanced age, he was likely never going to become director; unless, of course, something unnatural happened to Bryce—like a sculpture bashing in his brains, for example. I doubted the Colonel could manage it. He couldn't lift that weight and bring it down with enough force—not at his advanced age.

"Time to go now, Dodge," the Chief called over to me. "Don't wanna miss that train of yours."

"Train?" Lydia asked. "You're leaving?"

"They'll have to bring me back as a witness," I said. "Provided you plead not guilty."

"Of course," she said. "I'm innocent." I gave her a quick consolation kiss through the bars.

Elizabeth wanted nothing more to do with me; on the surface, Lydia appeared guiltier than hell; the Colonel never got around to authorizing me to stay on the case; and the Chief was giving me a personal police escort out of town—the job was pretty much over. I drove Monty's car to the train station. The

Chief followed behind just to make sure I didn't make any detours. He even made sure that I boarded the train safely, and waved goodbye to me as it pulled out of the station.

22.

Maybach: Dinner for Two

I HUNG ON ELIZABETH'S EVERY WORD as she revealed the poisoning scheme that Dodge had uncovered. Each time she mentioned Dodge's name I noticed a slight wince. It almost seemed as if she was in love with him, and hurting a great deal inside. But each time I tried to dig deeper into the subject of Dodge, she quickly guided the conversation to the cat show. With the murder suspect in custody, and her potential poisoner deceased, Elizabeth believed that she and the cat show were no longer in peril. I looked over at Dash and Lil and prayed that she was right.

We decided that it would be best to discard all the food in the house in case it was tainted. So Briggs and I went to the market. There was a plentiful, yet rather dull selection from which to choose. I always had this problem when preparing food in Olde Sayville. The spice offerings tended to be tame, supporting more of a meat and potatoes mentality. It was a perfect metaphor for the town. After a brief, and unenthusiastic shopping spree, Briggs drove me to the train station so I could collect my car. It was now five-thirty, and Dodge's train back to New York was long gone. My Mercedes was the only car left in the station's small parking facility. I asked Briggs to transfer the groceries to my car. Briggs was put off by the notion, and insisted that he could drive them back to the house and make sure they were put away properly.

But with all this talk of poisoning, I was adamant that the food not leave my sight. It wasn't that I didn't trust Briggs—at this point I didn't trust anyone. To alleviate the situation, I told Briggs that my distrust was of two certain kitties with purloining tendencies, and that they needed to be distracted while the food was safely hidden away. I'm not sure whether he believed me or not, but he dutifully helped me transfer the groceries.

Once inside my car, I opened the glove compartment. There was a note from Dodge attached to my car keys. "Pick me up at the South Sayville Heights station. Drive fast!"

◄ ◄ ◄

"IT'S ABOUT FUCKING TIME, MONTY," Dodge said as he approached the car. "Nice of you to show." I opened the passenger door and Dodge climbed in.

"You got anything to eat?" he asked. "I'm starving."

I motioned toward the groceries in the back seat. Dodge dug in and began nibbling on the first thing he could find: stalks of celery.

"Why the elaborate charade?" I asked.

"I was personally escorted onto the train by the Chief of Police," Dodge said between crunches of celery. "Little Napoleon wanted to make sure I left town."

"Why?"

"I guess you haven't heard about the Colonel," he said.

I looked over at him wide-eyed.

"Keep your eyes on the road, Maybach," he said.

"What happened to the Colonel?" I asked, trying to focus on the dusky road ahead.

"He's in I.C.U."

"Is he all right?"

"Looks like he'll pull through. He was almost breathing on his own when I left."

"What happened?"

"The official story is that I gave him a heart attack," Dodge answered.

"And the unofficial story?"

"Pretty much the same, actually."

"Phil, how could you?"

"It wasn't intentional. How was I supposed to know he was boffing Wanda?" he shouted out defensively.

"More big city humor?"

"Something like that," he said.

I reached over to the grocery bag and pulled out the first thing I could grab, which turned out to be a box of truffles.

"Shall I put the top down?" I asked facetiously. "We can dine *al fresco*."

Dodge didn't laugh at my joke. Instead he asked, "How's Elizabeth?" It appeared obvious that Dodge had strong feelings for her. Strong enough to bring him back to the dry town of Olde Sayville.

"She's well, I suppose," I answered, not knowing what else to say. Dodge stared out at the road ahead.

"Did she say anything?" he asked, without looking at me.

"Why, yes," I answered enthusiastically. "She told me about the jars of poison hidden in the trunk, and how Wanda—"

"You know what I mean," he said, cutting me off.

"You seem to be a sore subject," I said gently.

Dodge continued to stare at the road. His eyes winced a little, causing a rippling effect across his entire weathered face; his skin now resembling cracked leather.

"Why did you come back?" I finally asked.

"A few things didn't add up."

"For instance?"

"Why do you think Wanda would've wanted Elizabeth dead?" he asked.

"I don't know," I answered.

"Too bad," he said. "Cuz I sure as hell don't have a clue either."

"Perhaps someone was paying her to do it," I offered.

"Maybe."

We drove along in silence for a minute or so.

"Tell me everything you know about the Judge," Dodge finally said. "And this curse."

It wasn't an easy request. I first met the Judge when he was in his seventies, and didn't really know him, except from afar. But even from that distance, the Judge that I knew was starkly different from the Judge that was represented in the portraits and referenced in the context of Olde Sayville lore. To me, he wasn't some sober, scowling Puritan. He seemed rather relaxed, actually. He often wore an impish grin, not unlike the one Bryce sported. And as far as the curse . . . until this visit to Olde Sayville, I'd never witnessed the curse in action. It was always mentioned as a thing of the past, and I assumed, over time, whatever truth the legend bore had eroded into myth. I related this to Dodge as best I could. Thankfully, he listened patiently.

"What do you know about his previous wives?"

"Both died young. Cancer."

"Do you know what kind?"

"No," I answered. "Why would that matter?" I asked.

"It all depends who diagnosed and treated them, and what the symptoms were."

"Yes," I agreed. "But I have a feeling the attending physician is long dead."

"And so is Wanda. Watch the road, Monty!"

I had swerved a bit with a sudden realization.

"Is it possible, then, that Wanda was actually the intended victim?" I asked.

"Bryce took over from the Judge as director of the club. He had access to information that only the Judge would have had," Dodge postulated. "Wanda was the Judge's loyal servant her entire life. Imagine all the things she knew." He took a pause, then said forebodingly, "And Elizabeth was the Judge's wife."

"Aha," I said, seeing exactly where Dodge was going with this line of logic. "So whoever wrote those letters may really just be looking to keep the Judge's past from resurfacing. The cat show is just a ruse."

"Smoke and mirrors, Maybach."

I thought about the repercussions of these possibilities. If winning the cat show was not the true aim of the letter writer, and the motive far more sinister, that left the other club members in rather precarious positions.

"So Elizabeth may still be in danger, then?" I asked.

"Yes," he said. "And the way I figure it, maybe the Colonel, too."

"Why? Are you planning on giving him another heart attack?" I quipped. Dodge failed to see the humor, and continued explaining.

"The Colonel is the last surviving charter member," he said. "I'll bet he could tell some tales. And whoever becomes the new director will have access to the information that Bryce had access to."

"So whoever is doing this," I said, picking up on Dodge's innuendo, "is using the curse as an angle to kill off anyone who takes the directorship. The curse's legacy, as it were."

"Perhaps," Dodge said. "The big question is why."

Dodge seemed stumped at this point.

"Maybe the killer wants to eventually take over as director, so he can destroy whatever incriminating information that the director is privy to," I offered.

"Not bad, Monty," Dodge replied, seemingly impressed. "And by associating a curse with it, he figures people will be scared off from taking it on. Leaving it wide open for the perp to rise to power."

"So the Colonel's death would serve a triple purpose," I elaborated. "Firstly, it perpetuates the myth, secondly, removes another possibly incriminating link to the past, and thirdly moves the villain one step closer to the directorship."

"You know," Dodge said thoughtfully, "my putting the Colonel into I.C.U., under twenty-four-hour surveillance, may end up saving his life." He seemed pleased with himself. Or perhaps it was just his way of rationalizing.

I ate another truffle. All this intrigue was terribly exciting. It led me to wonder about Lydia. Had she been framed? Did the police actually have any evidence by which to arrest her?

"Do you think Lydia is involved?" I asked.

Dodge exhaled.

"The numbers sure seem to point to it," he said, staring at the road. "But after our little discussion right now, I'm not sold on it yet."

"But the police certainly are. That means it's up to us to find the true culprit, yes?"

"So it would seem, Monty," he answered half-heartedly, continuing to stare at the darkness ahead. Dodge didn't say another word until we reached the Olde Sayville border. He just rubbed his stomach.

23.
Dodge: A Toxic Relationship

I STRETCHED OUT IN THE BACK SEAT of Maybach's car. Monty was inside the Hathorne estate trying to talk Elizabeth into letting me back into the house. I knew it would be a tough sell, but Monty wanted to give it the old college try. My backup plan was to sleep in the car, so I was sizing up the leg room.

I thought about the case. Too many items still didn't add up. Lydia was arrested prematurely. The cops couldn't have collected enough evidence, and analyzed it in such a short timeframe; and with their track record for bumbling, it was pretty astounding that they got a positive match on the ballistics so easily. Perhaps someone wanted her arrested. And perhaps that person was the letter writer. It would then be reasonable to expect no more letters to surface. If one did, Lydia would be exonerated; but the letter writer wanted Lydia to take the fall.

Lydia's alibi involved Lloyd Proctor, and, according to both Monty and the Chief, he wasn't exactly a stellar witness. In fact, he still hadn't been seen by anyone since Bryce's murder. If the person who wanted to frame Lydia also got to Lloyd, her defense would be completely sunk. Lloyd seemed like the kind of guy who could be bought; the kind of guy who'd take a payoff to leave town so Lydia would be left to dangle on her own.

Monty rapped on the window of the Mercedes. I had been so deep in thought that I didn't even see him approach. I opened the door.

"She's amenable to your staying," he said. I felt a surge of warmth, until I realized that Maybach hadn't finished his sentence yet.

"But only for tonight," he continued. "She doesn't want to see you, so you'll have to wait until she's retired for the night before you can come into the house."

"Great," I said sarcastically.

"Also," Monty continued, "she doesn't want you anywhere in the house except the guest room."

"Anything else?"

"Yes," he said. "She wants you gone before she wakes up."

"If that's the way she wants it," I said, trying to be glib. "How long do I have to wait before I can go in?"

"Probably another few hours or so."

"I'm going for a drive then," I said, moving up into the driver's seat.

"Would you like me to convey any message on your behalf," Monty asked with a pitying look.

"Sure," I said. "Tell her she should pour herself a stiff drink and lighten up."

I slammed the car into gear and hit the gas. I had a few hours to kill so I paid a visit to a one-hour photo lab and waited around for my film to be developed. Even though the Chief was an admitted liar, I wondered if there was any truth to what he had said about Lydia's guilt and the ballistics results. If Lydia was really the perp, the pictures I took of the tire treads at the crime scene and of Lydia's Lexus would match up. I was hoping to put an end to the speculation and prove the Chief wrong once and for all. An hour later I looked at the newly developed prints. The tire treads from the crime scene matched perfectly with those from the Lexus. Unless they were planning to frame Lydia from the very start, this didn't look promising for her. I drove back to Elizabeth's place. Maybach was waiting for me on the porch— pale and trembling.

"What happened?"

Maybach broke the news to me. Elizabeth had been a jittery mess. Her chills had gotten much worse while he was preparing dinner. But midway through the first course, she said she felt suddenly feverish, complained of gastric discomfort and then began to vomit into her soup bowl.

"Had I not known about the poisoning, I would have taken it personally," Maybach said, trying to insert some levity. "Briggs rushed her to the hospital. He took those jars from the old trunk for the doctors to analyze."

I pushed Maybach into the car and we sped off to the hospital. Maybach and I charged in through the emergency entrance, where we found Briggs, waiting calmly.

"How is she?" I asked.

"It was quite frightening," Briggs answered, "but she's going to pull through. They pumped her stomach just to make sure."

I was so relieved, I hugged Maybach.

"Can we see her?" I asked.

"No, she's been sedated and she's in restraints. The poison was causing her severe itching. While I was driving here, she scratched herself so hard, she ripped through her skin with her nails. She was a screaming bloody mess by the time we got here."

"My God," Maybach said. "The poor dear."

I felt like a chump. I should have insisted on taking her to the hospital, rather than taking advantage of her; but I let my libido take over. Just like with Valerine Rizzo, I followed my dick instead of my head. Then I realized it was the poison, and not God's intervention, that was responsible for Elizabeth losing her inhibitions—yet another seeming miracle quashed with a scientific explanation. My self-loathing was interrupted by an annoying familiar voice.

"I knew you'd be back, Dodge. Just didn't expect you so soon," the Chief of Police said as he swaggered through the door.

"Have you seen her?" I asked.

"Yup. She'll be okay. Doc says no visitors 'til morning,

though, so you may as well turn around and go back where you came from."

"How's the Colonel doing?" I asked him. He just shrugged his little shoulders. "You never can tell for sure," he said. "I'd stay away from him if I were you, Dodge. You've already done enough."

✳ ✳ ✳

MAYBACH AND I RETURNED to the Hathorne estate, while Briggs waited at the hospital. I asked Briggs to call as soon as he received any word on Elizabeth's condition.

"I doubt I'll be able to fall asleep easily tonight," Monty said, as one of the cats leapt onto his lap.

"Being a detective," I lectured, "you've got to learn to sleep whenever the opportunity presents itself. It comes with the territory."

"And exactly, what would that territory be?" Monty asked.

"If you're on a case, you never know when you'll need to be on an all-night stakeout," I explained. "Maybe it's in some dingy fleabag motel room with thin walls so you can record what's going on on the other side; or maybe the window's got a nice view of your target. And you spend ten hours there waiting for one moment, when you can snap a picture, and that's your case right there. That one picture is enough for the target to agree to a large out-of-court settlement. But who the hell can stay awake and alert for that long with nothing going on? After a while, you get a feel for when you can steal forty winks."

Monty looked thoughtful for a moment. Maybe he could tell I was full of shit, and was about to call my bluff—the big, tough detective who's afraid of having nightmares about a twenty-year-old case. But when he finally spoke up, it was another subject completely.

"I assumed most stakeouts were in automobiles," he said, "following suspects around town, and watching their movements."

"No one drives in New York, Monty. And besides, there's nowhere to park. How am I gonna stake someone out when the closest spot is three blocks away? And with my rotten luck, just as the mark was coming out, I'd be busy moving the car across the street because alternate side was in effect."

Monty took it all in, then announced his departure.

"In that case, I think I'll be getting ready for bed now. We'll need to get to the hospital bright and early tomorrow."

"Quick question before you go," I said. "Did Lydia ever say what she was doing at Lloyd's house?"

"Apparently Lloyd had photos of Bryce and Elizabeth," he said. "She wanted them destroyed."

"How come?"

"To protect her husband's memory. That was her reason."

"Or to get rid of any evidence of her motive for killing him."

I showed him the tire tread photos. Then I told him about the crime statistics. He just shook his head from side to side. "But I've known Lydia for years," he said.

"You can't ignore the numbers, Monty."

"Yes. Of course you're right," he said. "Well, we've got a big day ahead of us, and I must try to get at least a little bit of sleep. Good night, Phil."

He turned and waddled up the stairs. I waited until I heard his door close behind him. Then I went upstairs and snuck into Elizabeth's bedroom. I fell asleep in her bed and had more nightmares about Valerine Rizzo. Except this time, when it got to the part where they pulled the sheet off the corpse at the morgue, it was Elizabeth's face on Valerine's body.

24.
Maybach: A Restless Night

MY MIND RACED. So much had occurred in the last few hours. But I still wasn't fully convinced of Lydia's guilt. Not just yet. I tossed and turned, sneaking peeks at the clock as I did so—it was two a.m. I flipped my pillows over and punched them, causing Dash and Lil to raise their heads from the foot of the bed and give me nasty looks.

"Well, what do you suggest?" I asked them rhetorically. Dash leapt from the bed to the bureau. He swatted at a balled-up foil truffle wrapper that I had left there, and knocked it onto the floor. Lil jumped to the floor and batted at it; then Dash jumped down from the bureau and batted it back to Lil. It was as if they were playing tennis with it. Were they trying to tell me something? Resident tennis pro, Lloyd Proctor, was the only one who could provide an alibi for Lydia.

Twenty minutes later, I was parked across the street from Lloyd's bungalow, watching the house. My first real stakeout. Somehow, I believed that Lloyd would return sooner rather than later—no one planning to leave town for any length of time would have such a well-stocked refrigerator; especially with so many fresh vegetables.

To keep me company, I had the remainder of my chocolates with me in the front seat. Sadly, I had underestimated my need for them on this trip to Olde Sayville. Dear Geoffrey always recommended taking less rather than more. "If it's so horrid that you need more to drink," he said, "it's probably best that you just leave the wretched place altogether."

As I popped the final chocolate into my mouth I wondered about Lloyd and Lydia. What sort of arrangement did they have? And if Lloyd really could provide an alibi, why wouldn't he come forward? Only Lloyd could tell us that. And I didn't trust Lloyd—no one did. It wouldn't have surprised me one bit to see him drive up to his bungalow under the cover of night, gather his belongings and skip town for good, leaving Lydia to fend for herself. If someone was putting him up to this, I wanted to find out who it was.

A car's headlights came into view from a distance, but then turned off toward another destination. I found myself scrunching down to hide myself from it, but realized that my large frame wasn't exactly suited to making myself invisible. I decided to perform my stakeout from the passenger side of the car, with the seat fully reclined, so as to keep my girth safely out of sight. I adjusted the rear-view and side-view mirrors to allow for optimal viewing of Lloyd's front door from my reclined position.

Another set of headlights came into view through the driver's side-view mirror. The glare from the reflection was temporarily blinding, but my sense of hearing was still intact. The car crept to a halt and parked in front of Lloyd's house. As soon as the headlights went out, I decided to ever-so-slowly raise myself up and peer out the window to see who it was—and if it was Lloyd, to confront the scoundrel. But unfortunately, gravity wouldn't cooperate, and I was unable to lift myself up. I rocked myself from side to side, hoping to gain enough momentum to launch myself off the seat one way or the other. I rocked left, then right, then left, then right, until I was able to lift myself slightly. It was enough of a lift for me to grasp the passenger door handle. A moment later, I was lying flat on my back, with a broken off door handle in my fist. Undeterred, I rocked some more, this time grasping the bottom of the bucket seat with one hand and pulling myself upward, while simultaneously activating the spring mechanism to release the seat from its reclining position. The combination of the two maneuvers propelled me into a sitting position. Breathless, I looked out the window and saw a Lamborghini parked in front of Lloyd's house. I looked at the front door and saw a silhouette pacing impatiently, before returning to the Lamborghini, and slowly driving off. But I couldn't see the driver. The obvious assumption was that it was either Eliot or Chip. Whoever it was had come looking for Lloyd, as well. Did he have the same inkling that I had? Or was there something else to this late-night visit? I decided to get out of the car and investigate.

I followed the same path as that of the Lamborghini driver, straight up to the front door. There was a window adjacent to door, but it was flanked by a rather large hedge. I moved it aside so I could get closer to the window and steal a look inside. But as I clawed through the bushes, I became the recipient of several thorn pricks. They ripped small holes in my clothing, but I continued on in my quest. When I finally reached the window, I peered in. There was no sign of life. It appeared to be in the same condition as when Lydia was arrested there the previous day. I clawed my way back through the hedge, pricking my index finger along the way. When I emerged from the bushes, I was tattered and bloody. I staggered back to my car and started the engine. My stakeout was officially over, and it left me with more questions than answers.

◄ ◄ ◄

I RETURNED TO ELIZABETH'S HOUSE around five-thirty in the morning and dropped off to sleep immediately. But after only a few minutes of slumber, I was awakened by the phone. It was Briggs. Elizabeth was doing much better, the side effects of the poison had waned, and she was scheduled to be released from the hospital as early as that afternoon, provided there were no further complications, and no signs of infection from where she had clawed at her own flesh.

"Excellent news, Briggs," I said. "We'll be there as soon as we can."

"Actually," Briggs said with a tinge of awkwardness, "Mrs. Hathorne has made it clear that she doesn't want Mr. Dodge around. Not at the hospital, and not at the house. She would very much appreciate it if you would make Mr. Dodge aware of her wishes before she returns home."

I heard a painful sigh, and then a click. Then I heard a door slam down the hall. I wasn't going to have to worry about breaking the news to Dodge; he had been eavesdropping on one of the extensions. I quickly ended the call with Briggs, and sought out Dodge. He was already downstairs, slumped in an armchair. He had tremendous dark bags under his eyes, indicating that he'd had a rough slumber as well.

"Phil," I said tenderly, but he cut me off immediately.

"Save it," he said, rising from the chair. "Let's get out of here. You can drop me at the club, so I can collect my money, then swing back and you can take me to the train station. I'm gonna wash my hands of the whole business."

"But what about Lydia?" I asked.

"The cops got their killer," he said. "As far as I'm concerned the case is closed."

25.
Dodge: A Going Away Present

AFTER GETTING MY MARCHING ORDERS from Elizabeth via Briggs, I set out for the Olde Sayville Society to collect my money. With Bryce dead, and the Colonel hospitalized, the most senior officer there turned out to be Eliot Stoughton. He was more than willing to pay me off; even seemed relieved that I'd be prying no further—so much so, his twitching dwindled down to a barely noticeable three ticks per minute. So my work for the Olde Sayville Society was officially concluded. I sat in the corner of the ballroom counting my money and watching the freak show. The preparation and preening that was going on in anticipation of the cat show was enough to make me physically ill. All this to-do over these spoiled bags of fur—that's really all these cats were; just sitting there all day long doing nothing except eating gourmet food, spitting hairballs and hissing occasionally. The fact that my intestinal backflipper was using my gall bladder as a trampoline didn't help any. The belly jumper should have been at rest—after all, the case was over and done with. But there were still too many loose ends. And the wee tumbler was active because I was about to leave town while Elizabeth was still in the hospital. I never had a chance to say goodbye to Valerine; and now it looked like I wouldn't get that opportunity with Elizabeth either. Just as I knew I would never meet another "Valerine," it was doubtful that I'd ever meet another "Hathorne." My mind began to race. What was the real deal with Wanda? Why would she poison Elizabeth? She couldn't have been in cahoots with Lydia. Lydia. No matter how much I didn't want to believe she was involved, the evidence and the numbers didn't lie. But how would Wanda fit in with all of it? Was she planning on eliminating Elizabeth all along, and used the letter writing campaign as an opportunity to strike? Or maybe Wanda was actually the letter writer and Lydia used that as her opportunity to strike? Lloyd Proctor's disappearance; Bryce's changed will; the Chief's admitted corruption; the directorship; the Colonel's sudden heart attack; Bryce's willingness to let the police handle everything, when it seemed—according to Maybach anyway—that he knew his own life was in danger; Elizabeth and Bryce's alleged affair; Lloyd's alleged photographic evidence; the golf tournament. It was all too much for the gym rat in my stomach. It couldn't all be attributed to coincidence, could it?

I decided to have a chat with Eliot, just to see if my suspicions could be assuaged. I caught him just as he and his first cousin, Blake, were heading out to the golf course.

"Too bad I have to leave today," I said, following them outside. "I would've loved to get some golf pointers from you."

"I'm hardly the person to give out pointers," Eliot said.

"Don't be so modest—you're the big champ around here, aren't you?"

"He sure is," Blake piped in. He had an arrogant smirk on his face—a cocky kid who was dying to spill the beans.

"I'll bet that surprised a few people, though," I said, offering up some bait.

"Heck, yeah," Blake answered. "You should've seen Bryce's face when Eliot sunk that putt."

"Blake!" Eliot cautioned. "Don't be disrespectful."

"There's nothing disrespectful about telling the truth," I said in Blake's defense. "If Bryce was surprised by it, he was surprised by it. It's not like it's some deep dark secret, right?"

As if on cue, they both forced a polite laugh. I continued to follow them to the first tee.

"Do you play much golf, Mr. Dodge?" Eliot asked, changing the subject.

"Funny thing," I said. "The only time I ever held a golf iron was to remove it from between some guy's shoulder blades. Gruesome business, I tell you. Gruesome."

There were no polite laughs after that one.

"But I've been planning to learn," I said. "I'm not as young as I used to be. I figure it's about time I started learning an old man's game."

There were no laughs from the twenty-something Blake or the thirty-something Eliot.

"Um, what time did you say your train was leaving, Mr. Dodge?" Eliot said, stammering slightly.

"I didn't. Why do you ask?"

"Well," he said defensively, "in case you needed a ride to the station, I'd be happy to–"

"I already have a ride, thanks. Besides, I wouldn't want to interrupt your golf game."

Eliot shrugged. There was a silence as Eliot placed his ball on the tee and lined up his drive.

"Hey, I have an idea," I blurted out as he was about to hit the ball. "How 'bout you give me those golf pointers now?" Eliot was startled, but recovered nicely after choking on some of his saliva.

"But you're not wearing the proper attire. You won't be able to get any traction with those shoes," he said.

"Don't worry," I answered, "if I end up losing to you, I won't use it as an excuse."

Blake snickered, machine-gun style. "I'd love to see this." He handed me a golf ball and one of his clubs—a big wooden driver. "Here. You can use my equipment. I'll caddy for you."

Eliot shot Blake a worried look, but it was too late. I had

already accepted the driver from Blake and placed the ball on the tee.

"Okay," I said. "What's the strategy here? No, don't tell me. Hit the ball with the club, perhaps?"

"But you're not even gripping it correctly," Eliot protested. But before he could say another word, I wound up and got ready to smash it. I thought back to my childhood days of playing schoolyard hockey back in Hell's Kitchen—when in my prime I could slap the roll of tape that we used as a puck into the garbage can that we used as a goal seven times out of ten. Pretending to be Andy Bathgate shooting at Jacques Plante, I whacked the ball.

"Beginner's luck," I heard Blake call out. I watched the ball come down on the fairway and take a giant hop onto the green, leaving it about twenty feet from the hole.

"Man, this is too easy," I said, prompting a sneer from Blake.

It was now Eliot's turn. He checked the wind, checked the sightlines, walked around the ball two or three times, very deliberately setting up his shot. He took several practice swings, then finally addressed the ball. I timed it perfectly. Just as he was about to hit the ball, I commented.

"Christ, Eliot. Just hit the thing. I've got a train to catch."

Eliot tried to abort his stroke, but it was too late. He pulled back slightly and the ball sliced into the rough about seventy feet away.

"Mr. Dodge," Blake shouted angrily. "You should never speak while someone is about to drive the ball. It's unsportsmanlike."

"That's just like in hockey," I said. "Except, instead of not being allowed to talk while someone is shooting, you're not allowed to punch him in the head, or trip him, or slash him with your stick. Not while he's shooting, anyway."

Blake was not amused, which was fine. This was purely for my own amusement. We set off to retrieve Eliot's ball. It was nestled in the tall grass. He shot me several dirty glances—as if I were to blame for his ball being there. He lined up the shot.

"What do you think about Lydia Danforth being arrested?" I asked. "Think she did it?"

"The police tend to think so," he answered.

"How about the letters? You think she wrote those, too?"

Eliot resumed blinking.

"Perhaps we can discuss this after I take the shot, Mr. Dodge," he said.

"Sure thing," I said. Then I folded my arms and watched him. A bead of sweat rolled down the side of his face. The pressure was on. He couldn't accuse me of sabotaging his shot this time. He took his swing, but he didn't hit it cleanly—he barely hit the top of the ball. It rolled forward about ten feet and died in a cluster of weeds.

"Tough break," I said. Eliot turned red. But not from rage—it was from utter embarrassment. "Good thing this wasn't during a tournament, huh?"

Eliot didn't answer. But he did continue to blink a great deal. He twitched his way over to his ball, and took another swing. It went about another ten feet. He followed it and swung again. And again. And again. Finally, the ball dribbled onto the fairway.

"When the hell is it my turn?" I asked.

"When you are the player furthest from the hole," Blake lectured.

"Oh brother," I sighed. "At this rate, I'm never gonna get to go." As we walked to Eliot's ball, I talked nonstop about how easy and simplistic golf was—just to be annoying.

"I don't get it," I said. "There's absolutely nothing to this game. No one's playing defense—I mean it's not like you have to get the ball past a goalie or anything. Where's the challenge? Even in miniature golf you have to time it so you get it past the windmills, right?"

The windmills comment caused Eliot to twitch and blink so much, I thought he was going to take off like a helicopter.

"You know what?" I said. "I don't think this is really the right game for me."

"I think p-perhaps you're r-right," Eliot said. Despite his stammering, he sounded incredibly relieved.

"Not now at least," I continued. "Maybe if I lost an arm or a leg in an accident, or if I were in a wheelchair or something, then maybe I could get into it."

Eliot twitched some more. Blake was now turning red—and not from embarrassment.

"You took one swing, Dodge," Blake blurted out. "And you got lucky. Why don't you just shut up already and go back where you came from."

"Lucky? You really think so?"

"Yes."

"You wouldn't want to put your money where your mouth is, sonny, would you?"

Blake's eyes lit up.

"You're on!" he shouted impulsively.

"No," Eliot called out. "Gambling is strictly forbidden at the Olde Sayville Society."

Blake quickly reversed course. "Yes, that's right," he said. "What was I thinking?" He stared at the ground. A long uncomfortable silence followed.

"So, still your shot, is it?" I asked Eliot. "What are we up to now? Five? Six? I lost count."

Then I got the look. The "I hate everything about you" look. I was glad I got it. Something to be remembered by as I waited out my final hours in this blue-blooded inbred freak show of a town. A nice going-away present.

"Much as I'd love to learn more from you about the intricacies of the game, I do have a train to catch. Thanks for those highly useful pointers, gentlemen." I emitted a smug grin of my own, turned on my heels and started walking back to the clubhouse; but Blake followed me. When he was certain that

Eliot was out of earshot, he renewed his challenge.

"How much, Mr. Dodge?"

"For what? Golf lessons?" I asked him as contemptuously as I could. "Just hit the thing hard and straight. No charge."

"You can't do it again," he said. "Not in those shoes. Not with that grip."

"I already did it once. What makes you so sure I can't do it again?"

"This time the pressure will be on you."

"Looks to me like you've made a wager like this before— even though it's strictly prohibited, huh?"

Blake refused to answer.

"Tell you what," I said. "Give me ten whacks, and I'll put at least half of them on the fairway," I said boldly.

"I don't think we have time for ten. Let's say two out of three."

"Doesn't leave a lot of room for error, does it?"

"That's why they call it gambling," Blake said with a demonic grin.

In the interest of full disclosure, let me just point out that I was absolutely truthful when I said the only time I'd handled a golf iron was to remove it from some stiff's spinal column. However, I had held a golf driver before. You see, after he retired, the aforementioned Andy Bathgate—the man whose slap shot was responsible for the introduction of the goalie mask— opened the Andy Bathgate Golf Centre, a driving range in Mississauga, Ontario. I made a pilgrimage up there every year or so. It was my way of giving back to Andy for all the thrills and great memories he gave to me. So even though I never gave a shit about golf, I ended up whacking several hundred golf balls every time I went. And since I couldn't care less, I never learned how to grip the club, and I always wore my regular shoes. I just stood there and pretended I was shooting at Jacques Plante.

"What do you suggest as stakes?" I asked.

"How about what Eliot just paid you?" Blake challenged.

"You're on."

Two golf balls flew onto the fairway. I didn't need to take my third shot. Blake started to weasel out immediately, saying that he didn't carry cash with him, and promised to send me a check the following week.

"Tell you what," I said. "Forget about the money. Just tell me why Chip threw the tournament."

The color flushed out of Blake's face, causing him to look like an anemic weasel. I could see him struggling to find the right words—whether he should go with an outright indignant denial, or just feign disbelief at the very mention of it. Ultimately, all he could muster was a little chuckle.

"Yeah, right," he said. "Don't worry, you'll get your money. I'm good for it." Then he grabbed the golf clubs and ran back toward Eliot. I knew I'd never see the money. That's how these guys stayed rich. Weaseling out of paying for things was their full-time job. Even though I wouldn't be receiving any compensation for my golfing time, at least it clarified a few things—there was no way Eliot could have beaten Chip if the tournament was on the level, and Blake obviously had a hand in putting in the fix.

I'd built up quite a thirst on the golf course, so I headed back to the clubhouse and entered the "cursed" office of the director of the Olde Sayville Society. I wanted to leave my lasting mark on the place by doing my part to uphold the pledge of temperance among the members. I decided to break into the safe and liberate the Scotch. In honor of Benny the Fist.

I closed the office door behind me, and proceeded to move the Judge's portrait until I stood face-to-face with the wall safe. I didn't care about leaving marks. The portrait would cover them up. I rifled through the desk in search of a tool; a letter opener, a ruler, a pen—anything that I could use to bore holes. I pulled the drawer out, flipped it over and dumped it. On the back of the drawer, I noticed that the wood stain looked peculiar. Upon closer inspection, I discovered three small numbers, cleverly etched into the stain. Nineteen, Twenty-Two, Twelve. Hardly noticeable at all. Nineteen, Twenty-Two, Twelve. I put the drawer back in the desk, and ambled over to the safe. I entered the combination, and the safe popped open. I ignored the stacks of cash, and went directly for the hooch. But on the way, I found an envelope filled with negatives. I removed the negatives and held them up to the light. They were of Bryce. And Elizabeth. They were going into a motel room. I shouldn't have been surprised by it, but I was.

I grabbed the decanter and noticed that there was ever-so-slightly less Scotch in there than I had remembered seeing the last time it was in my presence—maybe a quick swig's worth missing. Obviously, this needed to be investigated, so I took a swig of Scotch straight from the decanter, and checked the level again—about the same difference. Bryce couldn't have been too drunk when he got bludgeoned (unless he had finished the decanter, refilled it, and then drank it down again). I looked at the negatives one more time, then carefully placed them back in the envelope and cached them in my overcoat pocket. Elizabeth had lied to me. And deep down, I felt betrayed. I flashed back to the only time I thought I had fallen in love—my prom date with the Redhead-who-will-remain-nameless at the Fieldston School. I was a sucker then, but I was only a kid. What was my excuse now? I considered going back to Elizabeth's house and stealing the tuxedo—I could add it to my collection.

I took another swig of Scotch from the flask. My gastric gold medalist was finally at rest. And I felt much better about leaving town now.

26.
Maybach: Loose Lips Sink Ships

ELIZABETH WAS THRILLED TO SEE ME. She was weak, but definitely on the mend. They had just finished changing the dressing on her bandages, which were scattered over her arms, legs, hands and shoulders. I could still see traces of blood beneath her fingernails.

"It was unbearable, Monty," she said. "Like there were little bugs creeping inside my skin."

I had spoken briefly to the doctor. The lab analyzed the jars' contents and determined that the extracts were closely related to a family of poisonous mushrooms. He said that the itching sensation wasn't really a well-documented side effect, but hallucinations were. Thus the sensation of bugs under the skin.

"Do you know how the Colonel is faring?" she asked.

"I plan to visit with him as soon as I leave you, Elizabeth," I said.

"Monty, considering all that's happened, I think it would be best to cancel—or at least postpone—the cat show this year. Would that be horrible?"

"Considering the circumstances," I said, "not at all."

"Please talk to the Colonel for me. Ask him to cancel the show. As director, he has the power to do it."

"Of course," I said. Then we were silent for a few moments.

Originally, I had felt compelled to bring up the issue of

Dodge. But Dodge had requested that I meet him at the club and take him straight to the train station, so now it looked as if Dodge was going to be safely out of our lives. And perhaps her previous intimacy with him was caused by the hallucinatory side effects of the poison. I decided to let the subject of Dodge remain unspoken. Instead, I said goodbye and went to visit the Colonel.

◀ ◀ ◀

"LOOSE LIPS SINK SHIPS."

Those four words were the only utterances to pass the Colonel's lips for the first five minutes of my visit. "Loose lips sink ships." The Colonel was hooked up to a breathing apparatus under his nose, providing oxygen, and there were at least four intravenous lines flowing into him. Large machines monitored his vital signs, and emitted small beeps each time he spoke his four words. Rudolf hadn't left his side the whole time, except for meals and to catch a few hours of sleep here and there. He told me that the Colonel had said nothing but these four words since he regained consciousness. "Loose lips sink ships." And that was the answer he gave to every question I posed. Questions like "How are you feeling?" and "Are you comfortable?"

"Loose lips sink ships." Beep.

"I just spoke with Elizabeth Hathorne, Colonel," I said.

A pause. Then, "Loose lips sink ships." Beep.

"Elizabeth thinks we should cancel the cat show. She urges your approval."

The Colonel was silent. His face twitched, accidentally shifting the breathing apparatus from his nose to his chin. Beep. Beep. Beep. He gasped for air. Rudolf moved the apparatus back under the Colonel's nose, and he began to breathe more easily. The beeping stopped.

"Judge will turn over in his grave," the Colonel finally said with a raspy voice. I looked over at Rudolf who seemed as shocked as I was at his response. Then the Colonel began to laugh, then wheeze, then cough. When the coughing subsided, he segued into much softer laughter.

"Cancel it," he said giddily. "Cancel the cats. Now and forever." He laughed uncontrollably after that remark. The monitors beeped fast and furious until a team of nurses came rushing in and quickly injected the Colonel with a sedative. Soon thereafter the laughing and beeping subsided almost simultaneously, and the Colonel faded off to sleep.

᠃ ᠃ ᠃

AFTER MY STRANGE ENCOUNTER with the Colonel, I headed over to the club. The Colonel's behavior was certainly out of the ordinary—even for him—and his gleeful malevolence at the cancellation of the event was particularly intriguing. As I mingled with the members at the Olde Sayville Society, I realized that this was quite possibly the last time I would ever see them. Seeing as how the cat show had been called off, there were no longer any reasons for me to be there; either sporting, or professional. I decided to wait for Chip to arrive before I broke the news that the cat show had officially been cancelled. I wanted to see all of their reactions. In the meantime, I sipped lemonade and discussed golf and gormandizing with Eliot and Blake, who had just played a very abbreviated round of golf. They told me that Dodge was waiting for me in the office. He had collected his money from Eliot, and then withdrew. He really had washed his hands, and quite frankly, I was disgusted by it. He was showing his true mercenary colors. I returned my attention to Blake and Eliot. I casually mentioned that I had been to the hospital to see Elizabeth and the Colonel.

"So, do you think the Colonel will recover," Blake asked, then gestured toward Eliot, "or are we looking at the Society's next director?"

"Blake!" Eliot quickly reproached him.

"It doesn't appear as if the Colonel will be released from the hospital in the near future," I said, pretending not to notice the indiscretion of Blake's comment. "He's hooked up to quite a few gadgets."

"What do you think his chances are?" Blake asked. But his tone seemed to be one of curiosity as opposed to one of concern. Eliot's blinking increased.

"Would you like another glass of lemonade, Monty?" Eliot asked nervously, trying to change the subject. "I'm sure Blake would be happy to get us another round."

"Sure," I answered, picking up on Eliot's desire to speak to me alone. "That would be lovely."

Blake excused himself and went off to retrieve the refreshments. Eliot looked at me, blushing and twitching from embarrassment. The signs of his nervous condition were apparent.

"He's only a kid, Monty," Eliot said. "He doesn't mean what he says. I hope you're not too offended."

"Not at all," I said. I waited a suitable amount of time; perhaps five seconds, before revisiting one of the subjects that Blake had raised. "So what's all this about you being the next director?" I asked as casually as I could.

"I wouldn't give it much credence," Eliot answered, dismissing my remark out-of-hand. "Besides, Chip might have a thing or two to say about it."

"Really?" I answered. "How so?"

Eliot fidgeted. "Forget it," he said. "I shouldn't have brought it up."

"Fine, I won't pry," I said in a conciliatory fashion. "But would it be fair to assume that the next director of the club will be driving a Lamborghini?"

"That's a pretty safe bet," Blake said with youthful exuberance, startling me from behind. He handed me a fresh glass of lemonade.

"It's improper and disrespectful to be discussing this right now," Eliot said, now blinking uncontrollably. "Our thoughts should be with the Colonel."

"And Elizabeth, as well," I added.

"Of course," Eliot said, blinking and blushing some more, embarrassed by his omission. "And Elizabeth Hathorne."

I saw Chip coming through the door at that moment.

"Chip," I called out, and motioned to him to join us. He made his way over, all smiles.

After a brief exchange of pleasantries among the four of us, I proceeded to the task at hand.

"I was just telling Eliot and Blake about my visits with Elizabeth and the Colonel at the hospital this morning," I said to Chip.

"How are they?" Chip asked politely.

"They both appear to be in good spirits," I said.

Pleasant chatter among the parties ensued, about how wonderful Elizabeth and the Colonel were, and how we all hoped and prayed for swift recoveries.

"By the way," I said to the three of them ever-so-nonchalantly. "Due to the circumstances, they've decided to cancel this year's cat show."

I heard three deafening gasps.

🐾 🐾 🐾

THERE WAS GREAT FUROR AT THE SOCIETY over the cancellation of the cat show. Chip ranted on the phone, Eliot's uneasiness was on exhibit in the form of several new facial ticks, and Blake's usual youthful exuberance was transformed into downright hostility.

"We're tempting fate," I heard one member cry out. "The curse is sure to return," shouted another. The ruckus was enough to bring Dodge out from the office. It was a fitting time for us to exit. I motioned to Dodge that it was time to go.

"What's all the hubbub?" he asked when we reached the parking lot.

"Elizabeth and the Colonel decided to cancel the cat show. You won't be the only one leaving town today."

"Who else?"

"Why me, of course," I said as we approached my Mercedes. "There's no more banquet for me to prepare."

A loud shot rang out. Dodge grabbed his arm and fell to the ground, then took hold of my leg and hurled me to the pavement. Another shot. This one shattered the windshield of my car.

"Stay low, Maybach," Dodge said in a harsh whisper.

The doors to the club burst open as the members came streaming out to see what was causing such a racket. We remained on the ground for a few minutes longer.

"Okay," Dodge said. "I think the coast is clear, Monty." Chip was the first one to reach us, followed closely by Eliot. They helped us to our feet.

"Are you hurt, Phil?" I asked.

"Just a little nicked," he said, and showed off a hole in his overcoat where the bullet had passed through. His arm was bleeding. "I'll be okay." He looked up at the broken windshield on my car. "I guess we're both staying a little while longer, huh?"

"Yes," I said. "It appears that way." I looked up at Eliot and Chip. "We need a lift to the hospital."

"Of course," Chip said. "My car's faster, so I'll take Mr. Dodge, and you can ride with Eliot."

As we squeezed into our respective Lamborghinis, I realized that Blake Giles was no longer in our company.

◀ ◀ ◀

CHIP AND DODGE WERE A MILE AHEAD of us before we even left the parking lot. Chip's assertion that his car was faster than Eliot's seemed to have far less to do with the vehicle than with the vehicle's operator. Eliot was a rather cautious driver, to say the least. And there appeared to be a direct correlation between the miles per hour that the car was traveling, and the twitches per second emitted by Eliot. As we took the curves on the road at a leisurely pace, I observed fresh skid marks accompanied by the smell of burning rubber—Chip's signature. I wouldn't have minded the slow pace, except that I was unceremoniously crammed into the car, and my legs were beginning to spasm.

"Who do you think could have fired that shot?" I asked Eliot. Even though the speedometer didn't move, Eliot's twitching increased.

"Why are you asking me?" he managed to answer.

"You were in the club. Did you notice anything suspicious?"

"I'm sorry, Monty," he said apologetically. "I need to concentrate on my driving."

He focused on the winding road ahead and drove very deliberately. And he also developed a new twitch—a constant rhythmic tapping of his fingers on the steering wheel, which was beginning to drive me slowly insane. Tap-tap-scrape. Tap-tap-scrape. I looked over to see what was making the grating noise, and saw that he was wearing a band-aid on his index finger, which scraped against the leather steering wheel each time he tapped it. I returned my gaze to the road ahead. I no longer felt the need to question Eliot.

27.
Dodge: Making the Rounds

DURING THE TRIP TO THE HOSPITAL in Chip's Lamborghini, I doubt that all four wheels were on the ground at the same time. His intention, he said, was to get me the required medical attention as soon as possible; but I had a sneaking suspicion he was just afraid of my blood staining his upholstery—that and the fact there'd be that much less time for him to endure my questioning.

"Where were you when the shot was fired?" I asked. "You looked like you were the first one on the scene."

"That's because Eliot's so slow. He was the first one to the door, but I was the first one to get to you and Monty."

With my one good arm, I held on to the door handle as we took another curve at mach one. This was likely my only chance to question Chip without him being able to simply walk away from me; and based upon the speed he was driving, that opportunity was dissipating. Rather than squander it, I dove into a more invasive line of questioning.

"Were you very close to your uncle Bryce?" I asked him out of the blue, hoping to catch him off-guard.

"Of course," he said, fairly devoid of emotion. "Why would you ask such question?"

"Because he cut you out of his will," I said matter-of-factly. "Is that something that close relations do?"

Chip hit the gas. I had assumed that his foot was already on the floor, but I was mistaken. "My uncle's will was his business," he said dismissively. "Bryce decided to give his money to a worthy charity. Who am I to complain about that?"

A good response for sure, but an easy one to have planned and rehearsed. I moved on to the next subject.

"Why are you so upset about the cat show being cancelled? You've got to know that a bald cat has no chance, right?"

Chip smirked—finally a genuine reaction. "In this town," he said, "everybody has to have a cat. It's expected. So if you happen to be allergic to them—like I am—you end up with a bald one."

I forced a laugh. I wasn't amused, I was just trying to catch him off-guard again, and I was running out of time. "That still doesn't explain why you would give a shit," I said with a big smile on my face.

"What can I say, Mr. Dodge?" Chip responded dryly, his poker face once again intact. "I guess I'm just a traditionalist."

The tires screeched to a halt. We were at the hospital's emergency entrance. Chip abruptly ended the interview.

"Nice talking to you," he said as he jumped out of the car. He ran around to the passenger side and helped me out of the Lamborghini.

"Still glad you took me instead of Monty?" I asked sarcastically.

"Yes, sir," Chip answered blithely. "His extra weight would've killed my transmission."

★ ★ ★

THE DOCTOR PATCHED UP MY ARM, and gave me a prescription for some pain killers. Maybach waited for me, while Eliot and Chip decided to check in on the Colonel to see if they could persuade him to change his mind about canceling the cat show, citing the return of the dreaded curse.

"How's your arm?" Maybach asked.

"I've had worse," I answered. Actually, I hadn't. It was the first time I'd ever been shot; ironically it came on what was supposed to be my easiest job, away from the grit of the big city, in a wholesome, rustic, small-town "civilized" setting. And my arm hurt like hell.

"Whom do you suspect?" he asked.

"I don't know, Monty. I can't even think of a motive."

"Perhaps you were on to something."

"What would it matter? I was leaving town for good."

"As was I," he said. "But now we're staying." He looked at me as if he were making a point.

"So?"

"So maybe that was the intention," Maybach postulated. "This person didn't want us to leave until we uncovered the real truth."

"So he shot me? A fucking anonymous letter would have sufficed, don't you think?"

Maybach appeared to be deep in thought. "Perhaps, it would be a good idea if we tried to convince the Colonel to reinstate the cat show."

"Why? Afraid the curse will come for you next?"

"Don't be foolish," Maybach said annoyed. "Look, we can't have a banquet without a cat show."

"So?"

"So . . . at the banquet, we can lay a trap for the villain."

"Which one? This town is full of them."

"So it would seem," he said. "But I think I have a recipe that might lead to the discovery of our letter writer. Especially if we have all the suspects together in one room."

"Does that stuff really happen?" I asked. "I thought that was only in old detective movies."

Maybach ignored my last comment and excused himself to check on the Colonel. I was glad that he did. I walked down the corridor a few strides behind him. Monty turned into the

Colonel's room and I kept on walking. I spotted Briggs coming out of one of the rooms. I made sure he didn't see me, and waited until he was out of sight. Elizabeth had made it clear that she didn't want to see me ever again. Of course, she also made it clear that she and Bryce never had an affair. All bets were off. I swaggered into the room. There was Elizabeth, propped up in her hospital bed, bandages wrapped around her wrists—if I didn't know any better, I'd assume she had tried to commit suicide. She stared up at me as I entered the room.

"What are you doing here?" she asked.

I showed off the bandage on my arm. "Pesky bullet," I answered. I walked over to her bedside, and pulled up a chair.

"Mind if I sit down?" I asked. "I lost some blood, so I'm feeling a little light-headed." I sat down before she could answer.

"I'm sorry about your arm, Mr. Dodge," she finally said.

"I'll be alright."

"I know you will," she said. "The reason I'm sorry is that I was hoping never to see you again."

"I'm aware of that," I answered. I stayed seated at her side, and stared into her blue-green eyes. I wondered if I would fall victim to her "spell" again, even though I had the incriminating negatives in my breast pocket, shielding my heart.

"I came to apologize," I said.

"About Lydia Danforth?" she asked.

"No. Because I have no reason to apologize for that. What happened between Lydia and me had nothing to do with what happened between us. Just like you'd have no need to apologize for anything in your past prior to that night either, right?"

Elizabeth looked away. She seemed embarrassed. "Then what is it that you need to apologize for, Mr. Dodge?"

"I'm sorry I took advantage of you. It was unprofessional of me."

She looked back at me, her blue-green eyes piercing through me, trying to melt the negatives away from heart.

"The poison caused you to hallucinate," I continued. "You never would have done any of those things with me otherwise."

She looked furious. She grabbed my collar, pulled me toward her and kissed me hard on the mouth.

"The poison is most certainly out of my system by now," she said releasing me from her lip grip. "Damn you, Dodge." She kissed me again. "Why can't I control myself around you?"

And I thought I was the one with control issues.

"Call me Phil," I said, and then swooped in for a big kiss. The fog was returning, despite the damn negatives.

"I know the type of man you are," she whispered in my ear. "You're just going to break my heart again."

"You must have me confused with somebody else," I whispered back.

"You're a liar," she said gently nibbling on my ear. "You're not the settling-down, small-town type." She moved her lips from my ear to my mouth, and kissed me long and deep.

"You never know," I said. "Now that someone's trying to kill me, I almost feel at home here."

Elizabeth suddenly pulled back.

"Have you uncovered something?"

"Not to my knowledge. I pressed a few buttons back at the club, but not enough to get me knocked off."

"Like what?"

"I played a little golf with Eliot and Blake."

Elizabeth's eyes widened. I took note.

"What else happened?" she asked.

"I made an offhand remark about the integrity of last year's golf tournament," I said.

"Was anyone else around when you said it?"

"Nope, just Eliot and Blake."

"Perhaps it would be safest for you if you left Olde Sayville," she said.

"Trying to get rid of me so soon?"

"It's for your own safety."

"I couldn't agree more," boomed a smug little voice. I turned around and saw little Chief Napoleon leaning in the doorway.

"What took you so long?" I asked facetiously.

"Had to interview the folks at the club first," he said. He looked at Elizabeth, then back to me. "Hope I'm not interrupting anything."

"Make an arrest yet?" I asked, ignoring his last statement.

He smiled and shook his head. "Nope. May not ever solve this one." He continued grinning. "Perhaps it would be best if you took Mrs. Hathorne's advice and got out while you still can."

"Not while Mrs. Hathorne's life is still in danger," I said. Elizabeth stared at me.

"But Wanda is dead and Lydia Danforth is behind bars," she said.

"It's a lot bigger than that," I said. "I think your husband took a lot of secrets to the grave with him, and you're stuck in the middle." The Chief stopped smiling. "And this latest murder attempt proves it," I added.

"What the hell are you talking about, Dodge?" the Chief said through his gritted little teeth.

"It's all about the curse, isn't it, Chief? Someone's afraid that I'm getting too close. Just like they thought Elizabeth was getting too close."

The Chief fumed. "You've got no authority here, Dodge."

"If you have no official business with me, I would appreciate it if you left," Elizabeth said to the Chief. "Your presence is hindering my recovery. This *is* a hospital, after all."

The Chief bowed his head and offered his apologies to Elizabeth, then slipped out of the room. She grabbed my hand and pulled me close to her.

"Is it really true? What you just said? The curse?"

"I'm starting to believe," I said.

I didn't really believe it. But it was a way to get Elizabeth to stop urging me to leave.

"So you'll be staying a little longer, then?"

"Of course," I answered. "Blake owes me money."

"Blake?"

"Didn't I mention that? He was acting up, so I suckered him."

"You like to live dangerously, don't you, Phil?" she said with a playful smirk—it was the same expression I'd seen back at the house, just before she danced naked for me. I moved in for another deep kiss. At that moment, it didn't matter to me one iota that I found those negatives of her and Bryce. She pulled me closer and kissed me harder. I barely even winced when she accidentally clutched my bullet wound.

✳ ✳ ✳

AFTER I LEFT ELIZABETH'S ROOM, I checked on the Colonel. Monty had just finished persuading him to let the cat show continue as originally planned, and was off to break the "joyous" news to club members. I entered the room and greeted the groggy Colonel. As I suspected, Rudolf was no longer there to sit vigil over him.

"Where's Rudolf?" I asked.

"Stepped out," the Colonel rasped, burping each syllable. He was having trouble speaking.

"Has he been gone long?" I asked. The Colonel shrugged.

"Expecting him back any time soon?" Another shrug. He stared away, refusing to make eye contact.

"Seems strange is all," I persisted. "Seeing as Rudolf hasn't left your side up until now. Then all of a sudden . . . poof, he's gone." The Colonel chose to completely ignore me. It was time to grab his attention.

"Rudolf tried to kill me, Colonel," I said. "But for your sake, I'm gonna pretend it never happened. Provided you give me some information."

The Colonel immediately looked back at me. Our eyes

locked and then he sadly nodded his head in agreement. I had made a number of assumptions and now I needed them all confirmed.

"We'll start off with just 'yes' or 'no' questions. I'll make it easy for you. Blink once for 'Yes'; twice for 'No'; three times if you don't know. That way you won't have to worry about any loose lips sinking ships. Agreed?"

The Colonel blinked once.

"Rudolf is your son, isn't he?" One blink.

"And Wanda was his mother?" One blink.

"And that's why he wanted to kill me. He blames me for his mother's death because I left the house when I should have been there to protect her and Elizabeth. And now he blames me for your current predicament. Isn't that so?"

One blink.

"You and Wanda had a secret affair and Rudolf was the result, wasn't he? And the Judge was holding this over your head so you would do his bidding and keep your mouth shut?" The Colonel closed his eyes sorrowfully, then opened them after about ten seconds.

"Did that count as a single blink?" I asked him.

He blinked once.

"Wanda poisoned the Judge's first two wives?"

One blink.

"Was she in love with the Judge?"

Three blinks. He didn't know. I chalked it up to his own ego, and assumed that the real answer was 'Yes.'

"Were the Judge's first two wives unfaithful?"

Two blinks. No.

"Did Wanda poison them because of something they did? Something she disapproved of?"

Again, two blinks. He looked very angry. He stared at me, begging me to ask another question.

"Did the Judge know about it beforehand?"

One blink. He looked at me as if to say "getting warmer, Dodge."

"Did the Judge order it?"

One blink.

"The Judge had Wanda poison his first two wives, and fixed it so they were diagnosed as having cancer?"

One blink.

"Were you the diagnosing physician? Did you fix that for him?"

One blink.

"Because he was the one who controlled all of your fates? Not only could he arrange it so you and Wanda would never see Rudolf again, he'd cause a scandal so huge your precious reputation would be ruined? Is that why?"

One blink. His eyes were misty.

"But if you played ball, he'd bring Rudolf on as a Club employee, where you and Wanda could have full access to him?"

One blink.

"And all the while—the death of his wives—this just added fuel to the fire about the curse."

The Colonel moved his lips. He wanted to speak. I leaned in close to hear what he was saying.

"Bootleggers," he burped into my ear. "He came from a family of bootleggers. He wasn't even a real judge. The whole curse business—it was all a con." He took a gasp for breath.

"It looked like you had more on him, than he had on you."

"It was too late by the time I found out."

"Did Elizabeth know about this?"

"Certainly not when she married him."

"What about now?"

"Now? Who knows?"

"Did Wanda poison the Judge?"

"Loose lips sink ships."

"Answer my question or I'll haul in Rudolf."

"She never told me whether she did it or not," he gasped while blinking three times. "And I never asked her. Words are meaningless. It's actions that matter."

"Thanks for your time, Colonel," I said and turned to leave.

"Dodge," he called after me. "You'll leave Rudolf alone, won't you?"

"On one condition. You write out the real history of Olde Sayville for me. You can dictate it to Rudolf when he gets back. Then sign it. I'll be back in the morning to pick it up."

"And you promise you'll keep Rudolf out of all this?"

"You have my word."

"Thank you, Dodge. He's all I have left now."

"One more question before I go," I said. "You don't have to answer this one if you don't want to. Why did the Judge call you the Colonel?"

"As a reminder," he rasped. "That he had a kernel of information. If he turned up the heat, it would explode."

The Colonel was very unsettled.

"It's okay," I said. "He's dead now. Probably burning in hell."

"I know," he said. "I'm just afraid that I'll be seeing him again all too soon."

Then he closed his eyes and drifted off to sleep.

28.
Maybach: Slumber Party—Just the Boys (and the Kitties)

IT HAD BEEN QUITE AN AFTERNOON. While Chip and Eliot had no luck in trying to get the Colonel to change his mind, I was able to convince him in mere seconds. In private, I told him I had a plan to reveal Bryce and Wanda's murderer, and he immediately assented to allowing the cat show to go on as scheduled. When I told Chip and Eliot that the show was "on" again, they were deliriously happy, and thanked me profusely.

I prepared a luxurious dinner, highlighted by a lemon thyme grilled pork chop with celery mash, fennel and white beans. Dodge ate it with delight. We also drank my last two bottles of wine – an Austrian Sauvignon Blanc with dinner, and an Amontillado Sherry with *crème brulee* in the drawing room for dessert. I needed to get Dodge into an agreeable mood before I told him my plan to reveal the murderer.

"Elizabeth is likely to be released from the hospital tomorrow," I offered as a conversation starter.

"Do you think there was anything to those rumors about her and Bryce?" Dodge asked seemingly out of nowhere.

"Lydia said that Lloyd had photos, but . . ."

"But she's not exactly reliable, is she?" Dodge said, finishing my sentence.

"It would appear not," I said. I scrutinized his face. "What's on your mind, Phil? Why are you asking this now, all of a sudden?"

He produced an envelope and tossed it on the coffee table. It contained the negatives that Lydia said she was so very interested in obtaining from Lloyd.

"Where did you get this?"

"Found it in Bryce's safe," Dodge answered. "Bryce had already paid the piper."

"And the piper, in this case, would be Lloyd Proctor?"

"It would appear so, Monty. Looks like Lloyd got his big payoff and bolted town."

I thought about it for a moment. I still wasn't quite following the logic. "I'm afraid the wine has gone straight to my head," I apologized. "Could you please fill in the blanks for me?"

Dodge took another gulp of wine. He leaned back and pontificated. "Lloyd was blackmailing Bryce. Elizabeth was also in those pictures. Maybe he was trying to blackmail her, too, right?"

"It would seem to follow logically," I agreed.

"All of sudden, Elizabeth is shot at, and Bryce and Wanda are dead. Lloyd knows that the police will be investigating and the pictures and blackmailing scheme could be discovered. Not wanting to be implicated, he takes his money and splits."

I thought about Dodge's conclusions. It sounded plausible enough—it would certainly explain Lloyd's unexpected hasty departure, and his refrigerator full of fresh vegetables—but there were a few things that didn't quite wash with me. I wondered if Dodge's discovery of the negatives had led to the attempt on his life. And if so, who knew about it. I decided not to challenge Dodge at this juncture.

"Tell me, Phil," I began, "did you say anything that may have offended Blake Giles this afternoon?"

"I sure as hell hope so," he said. "I was trying as hard as I could to piss him off."

Luckily, Dash and Lil had retired for the night and were out of earshot of the profanity.

"I found it rather odd that he wasn't with Chip and Eliot right after you were shot, don't you?"

"It sure did seem a tad strange, Monty," Dodge said. He was silent thereafter.

"How was your chat with the Colonel?" I asked as another conversation starter.

"Revealing," he answered. "Did you know that the Judge was a big phony?"

"What do you mean?"

"He's not who he said he was. Wasn't even a real judge. Came from a family of bootleggers—I'll bet that was his angle in making this place a dry town. He controlled the supply of booze in and out. And he got a cut of every ounce sold."

"Outlandish! Do you think Elizabeth knows about this?"

"If she doesn't, she sure will tomorrow."

"Do you think his former wives knew?"

"Perhaps that's what led to their untimely deaths."

Dodge spelled out for me what the Colonel had told him about how Wanda had been the Judge's accomplice in murdering his first two wives, and how the Colonel fixed the diagnosis of cancer on each of them. A conspiracy that would be revealed tomorrow night as well.

"The big question I have," I said aloud, "is why would someone want to shoot you when they did? What had you uncovered? Or, to be more precise, what was it that they believed you had uncovered?"

"I wouldn't read too much into that," Dodge said dismissively.

"And why is that?"

He shot a glance back at me. His eyes told the whole story— a gaze that said "Trust me, and never mention it again." I sat and wondered for a moment. And then it hit me.

"Eureka!" I exclaimed. "I know whodunit!"

"I was wondering when you were gonna catch on," Dodge said calmly.

"It all makes sense now—the negatives, the blackmail, the will, the golf tournament." I was ecstatic.

"Don't get too excited," Dodge reprimanded. "We still can't prove a goddamn thing."

He was right. There was no hard evidence—all of it circumstantial. "That's why we need to set a trap," I said.

"I think Chip's a little too smart to fall for that," Dodge snapped back.

"Chip?" I asked quizzically. "You mean Eliot, don't you?"

Dodge grinned from ear to ear. "You think Eliot did it? That guy isn't capable of killing a cockroach."

"That may be true. However, if the cockroach were threatening his standing in the community, he would—excuse the lack of metaphor—crush it like a bug."

Dodge smiled. "Well," he said, "I guess that's how we'll draw them out, then—play them against each other, using the other as bait."

"Good plan," I said. "But what if they won't bite?"

"I'll scare 'em into it. Just leave it to me."

We finished off the last bottle of wine as we sketched out our plan of action. We'd play good cop/bad cop. There was really no need to discuss who would play which role.

🐾 🐾 🐾

LATER THAT NIGHT I pondered the situation. I had practically solved the case. All I needed was the smoking gun. And Dodge was in agreement with my conclusions—we only differed on who the actual culprit was. I looked over at Dash and Lil.

"It's a good thing you are both such prizes to look at," I said to them, "because you've been no help in solving this case."

And with that, Dash swiftly leapt off the bed and scurried out of the room. I had no idea he was so temperamental.

29.
Dodge: Not the Cat's Meow

I WAS SPORTING A HELL OF A NICE BUZZ by the time I was ready to go to sleep. Between the Scotch and the wine, and the fact that I hadn't had much to drink the past few days, I was pretty tight. I went upstairs and headed straight for Elizabeth's room. My drunkenness let me directly to bed and just as I was about to drift off to sleep, I heard what sounded like someone creeping up behind me. I quickly spun around with my hands poised for combat, and found myself looking right into the face of one of Maybach's cats. Out of frustration, I lunged at the cat to scare it off the bed; but the cat chose to fight me instead. It took a big swat and scratched me across my arm—the same arm where the bullet had grazed me.

I went into the bathroom to wash the blood off, and caught a glimpse of myself in the mirror. I thought about Elizabeth and what she said at the hospital. She was right. If she had really fallen for me, I was definitely going to break her heart. I realized that there was just no room in my life for her; for love—as if I knew what love was in the first place. If my feelings for Elizabeth were the same as those for the Redhead-who-will-remain-nameless, then it sure as hell wasn't love. It was just some poor city kid trying to fuck something above his station, or, to quote those coppers on the night of the prom, someone totally "out of my league." I hate to admit when the cops are right and

I'm wrong. But there it was, as plain as the scratches on my arm; the truth of the matter was that love had never found its way to Phil Dodge, not then and not now. So as soon as Monty's little stunt played out at the banquet tomorrow, I would be on the first train out of Olde Sayville, returning to my big bad city, and the big bad people in it. Or maybe a bullet would find its way through my cold heart at the banquet. At least that way it would spare my having to tell Elizabeth. Either way, she was going to have to pick up the pieces of her shattered life. Maybach was going to reveal the Judge for the fraud that he was, and as soon as that happened, she'd be linked to the scandal forever after.

When I returned to the bedroom, the cat was still there, waiting for me by the doorway. It looked me in the eye, as if daring me to follow. Monty had mentioned that his cats had assisted in solving cases before. And right now I was just drunk enough to buy into it. I took a step outside with the cat. It led me downstairs to the kitchen, then leapt up on the counter and pawed at the cupboard.

"That's it? You want food?" I asked the cat, as if it could understand what I was saying. The cat meowed, as if to say, yes, you idiot.

"You expect me to feed you? After what you did?" I pointed at the cat's scratch mark on my arm.

The cat meowed again. I gave in and opened the cupboard. The cat pawed at a package of cat treats. I tossed one to the cat, which it promptly devoured. As I sealed the bag of treats, I noticed the drawing of a cartoon cat family on the front of it. There was a papa cat, dressed up to go to work, carrying a briefcase, and a mama cat, wearing an apron, and serving cat treats to the papa cat, and baby cat. It was all very boring. I looked at the expiration date on the package. April 17: the anniversary of Valerine Rizzo's death.

My heart sank into my stomach, temporarily suffocating the gymnast. Monty's fucking cat had just solved the Case of the

Loveless Detective. The strange mix of booze was doing a number on me, and it led to yet another self-discovery. It was all about Valerine. She was the one who continued to haunt me. And it wasn't just because of the guilt I was feeling. As I searched my soul, I ascertained that the real reason I hadn't bothered looking for her ex-husband was because I was afraid of losing Valerine after the case was solved. I yearned to be around her, I ached for her when we were apart—it wasn't merely lust. It was love, dammit, but I could never admit it. So it was love, not lust, that had clouded my judgment and led to Valerine's death. And maybe that's why love was forbidden from ever finding its way to Phil Dodge thereafter.

The cat meowed again.

"No more," I said, putting the cat treats back into the cupboard. "That's enough for one night, don't you think?"

30.

Maybach: Preparation

THE MORNING OF THE BANQUET, Dodge insisted on going to the hospital first. Briggs dropped him off there, and then took me to the auto repair shop where I discovered that my Mercedes still was not ready. The only loaner vehicle that they had available was a twelve-year-old Plymouth with a wheezing engine. Every time I tried to accelerate, it cried out for mercy.

But I had no other choice. I had a great deal to accomplish. Plan a banquet, and provoke a confession. I took Dodge's positive review of my tomato and peach gazpacho to heart, and prepared that as the soup course. For entrée, based on Dash and Lil's devouring of the fish that I gave them, I opted for a lemon and black pepper seared cod served on grilled potatoes with a bed of herbs and shoots, finished with grapefruit and black plum vinaigrette. There just wasn't enough time to prepare *crème brulee*—besides, if all went according to plan, it was unlikely that the members would be in any mood for dessert after Dodge and I played out our little game. I immersed myself in my work, and by the afternoon a wonderfully elegant feast was prepared. So impressive was the arrangement, even I was amazed by my own work.

After the exhausting day of preparation, I returned to Elizabeth's house to dress for dinner. Dodge was waiting for me there. Alone. He was still wearing the same rumpled clothes.

"Hasn't Elizabeth been released from the hospital?" I asked him.

"Not yet. Slight setback."

"So sorry to hear it," I said. "What's the problem?"

"She's feeling depressed, so the doctors thought it best to keep her there one more night."

"Shame," I said. "I'd like for her to see us unmask her would-be assassin."

"Speaking of which—everything ready for tonight?" he asked.

"As ready as ever," I answered. "I just need to change into my tuxedo. I suggest you get changed as well. We'll need to depart shortly."

"I've worn my last tuxedo," Dodge said somewhat cryptically. He stood up and then dramatically dropped an envelope on the coffee table. "You may want to incorporate some of this into your little presentation tonight," he said.

I opened the envelope and read its contents.

"How did you get this?" I asked him, with wonder.

"I called in a favor," Dodge said.

I looked it over again and again. It contained the real history of Olde Sayville. And after reading it through, even I wasn't in the mood for *crème brulee*.

31.
Dodge: A Change of Heart

I HAD LEFT A MESSAGE for Chief Napoleon that I'd be at the hospital to share with Elizabeth some very interesting information I had uncovered concerning the curse. He was waiting for me when I arrived.

"What are you doing, Dodge? What's the meaning of that message you left?"

"I know all about it, Chief," I said. "The invention of the curse, and your department's involvement in it all."

He looked up at me. "I have no idea what you're talking about," he said through his typical shit-eating grin. "Maybe you should go on back to New York before you end up getting Mrs. Hathorne all upset for no reason."

"Looks like you need a little history lesson, Chief," I said. "I've been talking to the Colonel, and he's filled me in on the fact that Judge Hathorne wasn't really a Hathorne at all—that he was just a bootlegger, who conned the whole town for over half a century. Now either the police were in on it from the get-go, or you've got to be the dimmest bunch of excuses for cops that's ever existed."

His grin disappeared. (Perhaps the shit he had been eating had a lousy aftertaste.)

"Maybach and I are going to expose the real killer tonight," I continued. "We're also going to expose this inbred cesspool of a town for what it really is. If you've got any sense of self-preservation, you'll get on board."

The Chief nodded, then backed away. He turned on his heels and walked as quickly as his little legs would take him, until he was out of sight. I wouldn't have to worry about Little Napoleon bothering me for the duration of my visit.

I checked in on the Colonel. Rudolf was now back at his side. He had a cagey look in his eye. He knew that I was aware he was my would-be assassin.

"You have something for me?" I asked.

Rudolf produced an envelope jammed with paper. I read through it quickly. The truth was even more horrific than I had expected. I was interrupted by the Colonel's rasping.

"Do we have a deal, Dodge?"

I shook his hand. "We sure do," I said. Then I turned to Rudolf. "Take good care of him," I said, and excused myself.

It was time to visit Elizabeth.

"What brings you here?" she asked. She sat up in her bed and extended her bandaged arms. I immediately answered her gesture with an embrace, followed by a long kiss. Then I looked into her eyes—so trusting. I softened. I had to tell her.

"Look, Monty and I are going to expose the killer at the banquet. And a lot of information is going to come out that you may not want to hear."

"I'm a big girl, Phil," she said with a smile. "I can take it."

"I'm not so sure you can take it in front of the entire town, though. Your husband was not the man you thought he was."

"What are you talking about?" she asked wide-eyed.

I pulled the Colonel's confession from my pocket and showed it to her. She turned pale as she read it. I grabbed it away from her when it appeared she was getting physically ill from it.

"How?" she whispered. "How is it possible? How could I have been so blind?" She began to weep.

I held her and gently explained that it would be best for her not to be present at the banquet. She agreed.

"I have a confession of my own, Phil," she whimpered. "This whole business about Bryce and I having an affair ..." She couldn't finish her sentence. I waited patiently for the whimpers to subside, and reassured her that everything was okay now. But the whole time I thought about the negatives in my pocket. Finally she was able to continue.

"Well, the truth of the matter is, we almost did have an affair. After my husband died, Bryce and I spent a lot of time together; especially at the club. I was helping him with the transition as he took over as director. I was very lonely after my husband died, and in a moment of weakness, I agreed to go with Bryce to a motel in New Hampshire. We checked in, but before anything happened, I changed my mind. Bryce was hurt at first, but he understood. We had something to drink of course, because we were no longer in a dry town, but nothing untoward ever happened. And that's the honest truth."

"Why did you feel the need to tell me this?"

"I don't want to keep any secrets from you," she said.

I reached for the negatives and pulled them from my pocket. "Do you know anything about these?" I asked.

She held them up to the light and gazed at each of them—in awe. "How in the world?"

"You never knew about these?"

"No," she said.

"Lloyd Proctor took these pictures. He was blackmailing Bryce with them."

"Lloyd! I should have known. That man is a scoundrel. The Society has him on a generous salary for what turns out to be seasonal work, at best. You'd think he'd be grateful."

"Maybe that leaves him with too much time on his hands," I said. She looked at the negatives some more.

"But the circumstances—they were all so innocent in retrospect," she said. "Nothing ever happened." Then a worried realization. "My reputation," she lamented. She lost her grip, and the negatives fell to the floor. As I bent down to retrieve them, I noticed the scratch marks on my arm—the gift I'd received from Maybach's cat the night before. It immediately triggered memories of Valerine. Those same feelings were present now; it was undeniable. I grabbed Elizabeth's shoulders, and stared into her eyes. She was frightened and lost. Her whole world had just crumbled.

"Why don't you come to New York with me," I said, contradicting everything I had decided to do. "It's a great place to start over and remain anonymous. No one cares where you came from or what you did before."

More amazing than my impulsive emotion-driven statement was that Elizabeth said "yes" without any hesitation. And she was enthusiastic about it. Apparently, she really did love me. And much as I tried to deny it, I really did love her.

We plotted our escape from Olde Sayville. As an excuse for her absence from the banquet, we arranged for her doctor to release a statement advising that she remain in the hospital one more night. He was an old friend of the family and more than happy to oblige. And surely it wasn't the first time that an Olde Sayville doctor lied about the health of a Mrs. Hathorne.

I thought about Valerine. I never looked out for her best interests. Like Valerine, Elizabeth told me that her life was in my hands. I wouldn't take that statement lightly this time. So I was taking her along with me.

32.
Maybach: The Murderer Revealed

THE BANQUET WAS BUZZING. The coriander grilled shrimp skewers were a smash during the virgin cocktail hour, and practically everyone congratulated me on the triumph. Dodge sat in the corner. He claimed he was being watchful, but I could have very easily mistaken it for moping. It was almost time to sit down to dinner. Eliot clinked the side of his lemonade glass with a spoon to get the attention of the crowd.

"I'd like to take this opportunity to welcome you to the Olde Sayville Society pre-Cat Show banquet. First of all, please join me in thanking Montgomery Maybach for the incredible job he's done in catering the banquet this year." I nodded my head modestly to acknowledge the rousing round of applause. During that interlude, Chip began to clink his glass with a salad fork to steal focus from Eliot.

"As some of you may have noticed," Chip said, "Elizabeth Hathorne is not in attendance tonight. She so wanted to make sure that she was well enough to judge the show tomorrow, she's taken the extra precaution of staying one more night in the hospital."

"Yes," Eliot said interrupting Chip. "I've spoken with Elizabeth and her doctor, and both have assured me that she will be healthy, rested and ready to go tomorrow morning."

There was much applause for Elizabeth, while Chip and Eliot

stared each other down. It was apparent that each was vying for the director's position.

"And let us also extend our prayers to the health and well-being of our beloved Colonel," Chip said once the room began to quiet down. Chip bowed his head; Eliot and the rest of the room immediately followed suit. I wondered what exactly Chip and Eliot were praying for—as a vacancy in the directorship appeared to be their greatest wish. After a moment, Chip raised his head and asked the room to join him in a round of applause as a salute to the Colonel.

I glanced over at Dodge. He was motionless. His head was drooped downward, and he seemed to be staring at his shoes. I quickly ran over to him and shook him. Startled, he looked up at me.

"What?"

"Sorry," I said. "When I didn't see you moving, I thought you had been shot during the applause."

"Nah," he answered. "That'd be too easy."

I returned my attention to Eliot, who, not to be outdone by Chip in the praying department, requested that we all bow our heads as he led the Society members in a prayer. I bowed my head, but made sure to keep my eyes open. The prayer ended, and we all took our seats. When the tomato and peach gazpacho had been placed, I asked Dodge if he was ready.

"Sure," he answered.

I stood up and got the attention of the crowd.

"Ladies and gentlemen, friends and acquaintances," I began. "Despite some very long odds, we are seated here for this gala event." There were kind smiles and heads nodding in agreement. It was time to remove those happy-go-lucky grins. "But before we begin," I continued, "I'd like to take this opportunity to tell you that Lydia Danforth is innocent. Tonight, Mr. Dodge and I intend to set the record straight."

A few murmurs greeted my comments. I had been hoping for

a bigger reaction.

"Did I mention that the real murderer is sitting in this room among us?" I added nonchalantly. This produced the reaction that I sought. Very audible gasps. Even a stifled scream. With this newfound sense of accomplishment, I continued.

"To better understand the situation, I must bring a few facts to light. The first of these facts involves Lloyd Proctor, who has been quite visibly absent these last few days. Lloyd is known around here as the Society's resident tennis pro; but he is more than that. He is also a gossip and a blackmailer."

Far fewer gasps this time. Apparently this news was less than earth-shattering. I continued.

"The recent flurry of poisoned pen letters had nothing at all to do with the curse. It was actually an elaborate game of blackmail that spiraled out of control. And the author of these poisoned pen letters was none other than Lloyd Proctor. What made this particularly tricky was that the target for his blackmail wasn't Elizabeth Hathorne—he was blackmailing Bryce Danforth."

Everyone began buzzing, whispering among themselves. Finally, Chip spoke up.

"But why, Monty? Why would he kill Bryce?"

"I never said that he killed anyone," I answered. "All I said was that he was the author of the letters."

The crowd gave a collective gasp and then hushed itself, almost in unison. I surveyed the faces in the room; all staring intently at me, awaiting my next word. All except Dodge, who lifted his slouched head and spoke up.

"There's a little bit of background that needs to be explained first. Your charming Chief of Police was kind enough to give Monty and me a history lesson a couple of days ago."

"Yes," I said, just like we rehearsed. "But what he failed to mention was that it was revisionist history." I took a dramatic pause. There was total silence. Until Dodge broke it again.

"Back in New York where I come from," Dodge said, "closet space is at a premium. Just too valuable to clog up with skeletons. So, it's time for a spring cleaning, even though it's about fifty years too late."

I could feel the tension in the room. Dodge was playing his part to the hilt. Scaring the living daylights out of anyone who had anything to hide—and in Olde Sayville, that was practically everyone. I attempted to ease the tension slightly.

"Let me begin," I said, "by saying that no one in this room can be blamed for what took place fifty years ago. Every single person in this room, either hadn't been born yet, was merely a child, or wasn't even living in Olde Sayville at the time."

"See? Not to worry," Dodge interrupted. "There's always a fall guy—a scapegoat that you can convince yourselves is the sole reason for any questionable acts or deeds that you may have committed. And Monty's gonna deliver one to you."

Dodge dropped his head back down, as if the proceedings didn't interest him in the least. All eyes shifted to me. I cleared my throat and began my talk.

"In 1692, twenty men and women were executed for witchcraft in Salem, Massachusetts. One of the three judges who passed these death sentences was Judge John Hathorne. In 1711, all twenty victims were exonerated. About thirty years later, many of the persecutors, as well as their descendants, left Salem and founded Olde Sayville."

"Yes, we know that, Monty," someone called out.

"But did you also know," I said, "that neither Judge John Hathorne, who died in Salem in 1717, nor any of his descendants ever made it here? The first appearance of a Hathorne in Olde Sayville did not occur until the twentieth century."

The room buzzed a little. I continued. "And what's more, the first instance of the supposedly centuries-long Hathorne family curse did not occur until the twentieth century."

More buzzing. "And there is a very good reason for that," I

said, pausing for effect. "The person who you knew as Judge Hathorne, wasn't a Hathorne at all!" I finished my sentence with a flourish. I opened up the Colonel's confession and read it aloud to the stunned membership. It explained that the Judge's real identity was Johnny Maurier, and he came from a family of bootleggers, who made their fortunes during Prohibition. Johnny Maurier was only a child at the time, but his father often took him on booze runs across the Canadian border. He idolized his father and vowed to be just like him and join in the family business. But when Prohibition was repealed, the family business was no more. That didn't stop the little Johnny. He remembered passing through a small town during one of the runs to Canada. His father, suspecting that federal agents may have been waiting for him on the main road, took an alternate route which took him right through the center of Olde Sayville. That's when the Johnny Maurier learned about the town's Puritan heritage, and he never forgot it. Some years later, he came to town masquerading as a descendant of the most Puritanical of the Salem judges, Judge John Hathorne, and easily fell into the role of instilling the lost Puritan values upon the town's populace. He fought to make the town dry, and succeeded. Now he would be able to emulate his father. He controlled all illegal shipments of alcohol in and out of Olde Sayville. Because the town-folk were outwardly supportive of the dry measures, but inwardly craved their alcohol, the ersatz Judge was able to set up a secret network that kept all the denizens supplied with alcohol, but scared to death of being exposed. That's when he realized he could make even more money through blackmail.

But soon the blackmail was beginning to wear thin, and there were some rumblings about making Olde Sayville a "wet" town once more. Within a year, it was legal to serve alcohol again. That's when Maurier discovered the power of the curse.

I paused. I looked out into the crowd. Horrified faces stared back at me. And behind the horror, was embarrassment. It was beginning to make sense to them now. Once they were over their embarrassment, I knew it would turn to anger. It was a lucky thing Elizabeth wasn't here. She could very well be their target. I continued reading.

The next part of the confession told how the Colonel became involved with Maurier's crooked scheming. The Colonel had just finished medical school and was about to get married to his high school sweetheart. But he had been secretly having an affair with the daughter of his father's housekeeper—Wanda Williams. And when Wanda became pregnant, the Colonel sought the advice of the person in the town with the highest moral character. He was under the false impression that this was the Judge. Maurier seized the opportunity. He arranged for Wanda to come and work for him, so she could have her baby in secret, while the Colonel went on with his wedding as planned. Once the child was born, and the Colonel was wedded to his wife, Johnny Maurier had all the ammunition he needed for a life-long game of blackmail.

Maurier's wife knew nothing about his real identity, or his real motives. It wasn't something he ever shared with her. She married him for his alleged virtue. While she fit the part of a Judge's esteemed wife to a tee, Maurier found her to be rather prudish, and less than adequate as a bedroom partner. So he began making sexual advances on Wanda. He held the child over her head. If she complied, the child would be well-cared for at a nearby orphanage; but if she refused him, he'd be sent away where she'd never see him again. Wanda complied. Everything she did for the rest of her life, she did for her child. Her Rudolf. That included poisoning Maurier's suspicious wife, at his request, of course. And with the Colonel being the attending physician, he stated that she had late-stage cancer that had gone undiagnosed for years. Maurier quickly remarried, but his new bride was dead within six months. The curse was brewing. But Maurier didn't limit the curse to his own family. It was all well and good to have a dreaded curse at his disposal, but it wasn't effective unless it had the potential to afflict everyone in Olde Sayville. So he arranged for the Colonel's father to have a mysterious boating accident. Then he poisoned Bryce Danforth's mother. The Colonel was on hand each time to attribute the deaths to anything but foul play, with the local police department quick to concur. Playing the part of the sober Judge, Maurier warned the citizens that the curse would eventually find them all unless serious measures were taken to make the town "dry" again. Frightened of this supernatural retribution, alcohol was banned once more, and Maurier resumed his bootlegging activities. No more incidences of the curse ever appeared. I held up the confession for all to see, displaying the Colonel's signature. Then I neatly folded the pages and placed them in my pocket.

"So for those of you scoring at home," Dodge called out, "that makes four lives claimed by your so-called curse."

"And it is my belief," I added "that the so-called Judge did not die of natural causes. He was actually slowly poisoned by Wanda, in a similar fashion to the way she poisoned his previous wives."

"Five lives," Dodge called out. "Chalk up another one."

"And, had Wanda not been killed," I continued, "she would have poisoned Elizabeth, too."

"Wanda makes six," Dodge said. "Add one more for Bryce Danforth, and that makes for lucky seven."

The crowd seemed numb.

"What does this have to do with Lloyd?" asked a perplexed club member.

"After the Judge's death," I answered, "Elizabeth felt certain needs. Bryce took over as director of the Society, and ended up spending a great deal of time with Elizabeth. Soon after, they planned to have an affair. Lloyd followed them and took incriminating photos. He threatened Bryce that he'd expose them if he didn't pay him for the negatives. Bryce refused. So Lloyd became Lydia's new tennis partner. He got close to Lydia and eventually told her about the photos. But Bryce still refused Lloyd's blackmail demands. So Lloyd devised the letter writing scheme." I paused to let it sink in.

"I'm sorry, but I'm not following any of this," Eliot said.

"Let me spell it out for you," said Dodge, rising from his seat. "Lloyd needs to make his little photos worth a lot more to Bryce, so he'll pay up for them. So he befriends Lydia, and tells her about the affair between Bryce and Elizabeth. This gives Lydia a motive in case a murder should occur. He dredges up the curse to threaten Elizabeth, as she is the new object of Bryce's affection. With his newfound access to Lydia, he's able to use her car without her knowing about it; which also happens to give him access to Lydia's gun in the glove compartment."

I looked around the room, making certain that Dodge's words had sunken in. We were throwing quite a bit of information at the audience, and if our trap was going to be successful, it was imperative that we didn't lose anyone along the way.

"So Lloyd's plan is manifold," I continued. "In order to convince Bryce to pay the blackmail money, he began the letter writing campaign, which Bryce countered by hiring Dodge to guard Elizabeth. Now it was Lloyd's turn to raise the stakes. After he had provided a motive for Lydia, and positioned himself as Lydia's only alibi, Lloyd attempted to kill Elizabeth with Lydia's gun. But that still didn't scare Bryce enough to pay for the negatives. So Lloyd arranged for the catnapping of Gaston. He kept Lydia away from the house by talking her into a second set of tennis, while Lloyd's accomplice snatched Gaston."

"We'll talk about the accomplice later," Dodge interrupted. "In great detail." He stared down the audience. I half-expected the guilty party to run screaming from the room. But, as that was not the case, I continued.

"The Gaston incident was the final straw," I said. "Bryce decided that it was time to put an end to these dealings once and for all. So he arranged a meeting with Lloyd early the next morning: the money in exchange for the cat, and the negatives. Bryce had asked me to come by the club early that morning. I surmise that he wanted me to witness the transaction—perhaps he thought that way he could avoid paying the blackmail then."

"But Lloyd knew Bryce might try something like that," Dodge interrupted on cue, "and arrived earlier than expected. So, with no witnesses, Bryce had to pay off Lloyd. Then he locked the negatives in his safe, and reclaimed possession of Gaston. The transaction was completed and Lloyd left the club." Dodge stared down the audience again. "And Bryce Danforth was still alive."

"Then who killed Bryce?" Chip asked, looking right back at Dodge, seemingly unfazed by Dodge's intimidation.

"We'll get to that in a moment," I said, putting an end to their staring contest. "Bryce's death wasn't part of Lloyd's plan. In fact it was the worst result possible. When Lloyd found out that Bryce was murdered, he feared that an investigation would reveal the negatives. Since he had already told Lydia about them, she might be able to implicate Lloyd in Bryce's murder—even though he had nothing to do with it. But to acquit himself of the murder charge, he would have to confess to the lesser crime of blackmail, which would have put an end to his tenure at Olde Sayville. Lloyd was desperate to cover his tracks—and he realized that he was still in possession of Lydia's gun. And he planned to use it on Elizabeth Hathorne. If the negatives were found, it gave Lydia a motive for both of their deaths. So Lloyd waited for Dodge and me to leave the Hathorne estate, and then shot at Elizabeth through the window. But he hit Wanda instead. He dropped Lydia's gun where the police were easily able to find it. They implicated Lydia, just as he had planned, and then Lloyd quickly disappeared from town."

"We'll find him," shouted a member from the back of the room.

"Doubtful," Dodge said. "He's got a three-day head start, and a boatload of cash that he'd just taken from Bryce. Besides, by killing Wanda, he ended up saving Elizabeth's life. When the letters first arrived mentioning the curse, Wanda saw this as her big chance to get out of the Hathorne prison where she'd been serving a life sentence. She could knock off Elizabeth, knowing that the letter writer would be blamed; or, better yet, it would be attributed to the return of the curse. Then she'd be free to spend the rest of her days with Rudolf. She had already begun the poisoning, and Elizabeth would have been dead in another forty-eight hours had Lloyd not interrupted her."

I took inventory of the room, looking for a hint of a guilty look from someone. But all I saw was a collection of pale, sickly faces. I definitely made the right decision in opting to forego the *crème brulee.*

"So we know that Lloyd killed Wanda," I said slowly making sure they were all keeping up. "We now need to determine who killed Bryce." I took a sip of lemonade while the room perked up a bit and buzzed anew. "Bryce wasn't the only person that Lloyd was blackmailing," I continued. "It is my belief that Lloyd had possessed some sort of illicit information on practically everyone in this room. But tonight, we'll focus on Chip Danforth, Eliot Stoughton and Blake Giles. Lloyd knew that the three of them conspired to throw the golf tournament, so that Chip would lose to Eliot in the final round."

Gasps and finger pointing ensued, followed by half-hearted denials from Blake, Chip and Eliot.

Dodge pounded home the point. "Blake found a sucker to bet with and put a load of money on Eliot," he shouted over the trio's protestations. "Then the three of them split the winnings. That sucker was Bryce Danforth."

"And that," I explained, "was one of the reasons that Bryce initially refused to pay the blackmail money. He had just lost so much to the Blake that he didn't have enough cash available to pay off Lloyd."

"You have no proof," Chip stated calmly. "Why would I want to throw the tournament and cheat my own uncle?"

"Because he had just cut you out of his will," Dodge snapped back. "You'd look like a heartless prick if you complained about the money going to a worthy charity, so you came up with this scheme so you could take what you thought was rightfully yours!"

More finger pointing and self-righteous shouting. By now, Eliot's blinking had gotten completely out of control. Predictably, he was the first to cave in.

"Okay, sure," Eliot said, "we made the bet, but that doesn't mean we killed him. Why would we?"

"Because Lloyd Proctor," I said, "being an athlete himself, could see right through your scheme. Lloyd threatened to tell Bryce about it if you didn't give him a cut of the earnings. And when Lloyd needed an accomplice to grab Gaston while he played tennis with Lydia, he knew he could count on one of you gentlemen to do it."

I took a deep breath. I was about to lay the trap. "But here was the problem: the other two weren't made aware of it. So, after golf conspirator number one helped to grab the cat, golf conspirator number two spotted Lloyd meeting with Bryce very early that morning, and assumed that Lloyd had revealed the scheme to Bryce. So golf conspirator number two snuck in and killed Bryce with the nearest weapon he could find—the sculpture of the Judge. He even threw over the wheelchair to make it look like there'd been a struggle. Knowing that Lloyd had been in the room recently, he hoped that the evidence collected would point to Lloyd. But instead, the police botched the crime scene. Meanwhile, conspirator number one—the catnapper—likely assumed that Lloyd had killed Bryce and then left town, but didn't wish to tell the investigators about it for fear that the golf conspiracy would be exposed." It was time to lay the trap. I delivered the next sentence with urgent clarity. "That leaves golf conspirator number three perfectly innocent regarding the murder of Bryce Danforth."

"That would be me!" Blake shouted. "I had nothing to do with it."

"N-no, it's me," Eliot stammered, and twitched.

"No, I'm number three," Chip avowed.

"No volunteers for numbers one and two, huh?" Dodge asked. The three fell silent and just stared suspiciously at one another. The game had begun. We had successfully turned them against one another.

"Confessing to being Conspirator number one wouldn't be so bad," Dodge offered. "At least you wouldn't be a murderer then; just a cat thief. And maybe an obstruction charge thrown in for good measure, but you'd be out in no time at all." He looked directly at Chip. "But that wouldn't be you, Chip. Being as you're allergic to cats, there's no way Lloyd would have asked you to do it."

"I'm innocent," Chip said defiantly. "I'm number three."

Blake and Eliot each gave Chip a long hard look. In the meantime, the rest of the members had risen from their seats and formed a circle around them. There would be no escape when the true culprit was revealed.

"How about you, Eliot?" I asked. "I see you have a band-aid on your finger. What happened?"

"I c-cut myself in the garden," he answered.

"That's almost a true statement," I answered. "But to be exact, you pricked it on Lloyd's hedge at around four in the morning."

Eliot's eyes widened in disbelief. He wasn't expecting that from me. "What were you doing there?" I asked, following up.

"N-n-nothing. We were supposed to play golf earlier that day and he never showed up. I got worried."

"Worried?" I asked. "About what? That he might turn you in

for murdering Bryce?"

Eliot turned beet red. His stuttering picked up and he was barely understandable.

"N-n-n. I d-d-d."

He stuttered and stammered and twitched and got redder and redder, until he froze up, took a deep breath, and finally blurted out, "W-we were going to rig the cat show. That's why. I didn't kill anyone."

If Eliot had admitted to killing the Lindbergh baby, there would have been much less venomous hatred directed toward him. The cat show was sacred. The Society members were ready to burn him at the stake for heresy.

"I was going to try to talk him out of it!" Eliot insisted. But his pleas were falling on deaf, and rather angry, ears.

At that moment, as if on cue, the Chief of Police, flanked by his entire police force, entered the room. Their guns were drawn.

"Stay right where you are!" he shouted, even though no one was moving at the time. "We just found Lloyd Proctor," he calmly announced. There was a hush and a lull as the room bristled with anticipation.

"And has he revealed the murderer to you?" I asked.

"Sort of," he said. "Not so much in what he said, though. You see, he's dead. We found him in the trunk of his car." The Chief leveled his gun and aimed it right at Blake. "In your garage, son."

Even I gasped when I heard this. It wasn't at all what I was expecting. I falsely assumed that the curse's death toll had ended at seven lives.

"Blake, how could you?" Eliot asked.

"You've got the right to remain silent," the Chief began, and continued to read Blake his rights.

A club member immediately ran over to Blake and placed his hand over Blake's mouth.

"Don't say a word, Blake," he offered. "I'll be your

attorney."

The Chief handcuffed Blake and led him outside. The Chief looked at Dodge on the way out. "Thanks for that little tip you gave me," he said. "I can handle the rest from here."

Dodge stared at his feet, avoiding eye contact. He suggested that I follow him into the office. But there was one bit of unfinished business I had to deal with. I clinked the side of my glass until the room settled down.

"You may begin the soup course," I announced. *"Bon appétit."* Then I followed Dodge into the office. He was completely out of sorts, and looked extremely troubled.

"How could we have been so wrong, Monty?" he asked.

"I know. I was so certain it was Eliot."

"Not just that," Dodge said. "Lloyd couldn't have killed Wanda."

He was right. I realized that there were now a slew of unanswered questions, and gaps of logic that needed to be explored.

"Yes, I see that now," I answered pensively.

We stood there in meditative silence until Dodge finally spoke. "You know what I think happened?" he said. "Part of the arrangement between Bryce and Lloyd must have been to return Lydia's gun, so it couldn't be used as evidence for that shot he fired at Elizabeth. So, after Blake snuck up on Bryce and caved in his skull with the sculpture, he pried the gun out of Bryce's dead hand, which would explain the broken fingers. Then Blake panicked, sought out Lloyd and shot him. He tossed the body in Lloyd's car, then stole the car to make it look like Lloyd had left town. He hid the car and the corpse in his garage, and then took a shot at Elizabeth to try and frame Lydia for the murders. And Blake is just cocky enough to think he could get away with it."

"Sounds reasonable enough," I said. "That would also explain why Lloyd had a refrigerator full of fresh vegetables. He had no intention of leaving town."

As it turned out, we didn't miss the mark by much after all. We just needed a slight adjustment to our crime-solving logic here and there.

"The toughest thing about all this, though," Dodge said with a pained expression, "is that the goddamn police figured it out before we did."

The very thought caused me to shudder. Dodge walked over to the safe and dialed the combination. He pulled out a flask and placed it in his coat pocket.

"Souvenir," he said. "How about giving me a lift to the station?"

🐧 🐧 🐧

WHEN THE SPUTTERING PLYMOUTH finally reached the station, I was surprised to see Elizabeth waiting for us there with a suitcase.

"She's coming with me, Monty," Dodge said blushing. It was the first genuine smile I'd ever seen out of Dodge. "You understand, of course, why she couldn't be at the banquet."

"You rascals!" I said. "Well, I wish you both all the luck and happiness in the world."

"Thank you, Monty," Elizabeth said giving me a kiss on each cheek. "So tell me, what happened at the banquet?"

"Blake's in custody," Dodge answered. "And the cops found Lloyd Proctor's body on Blake's premises, to boot."

"My God," she gasped. "Lloyd, too?"

I recounted the events of the banquet to Elizabeth, which adequately filled the time while we waited for the train. When I saw it approaching the station, I gave Elizabeth a big hug and then extended my hand to Dodge.

"A pleasure, Mr. Dodge," I said.

"Call me Phil," he said as he took my hand and gave it a firm handshake. I noticed some scratch marks on his arm as we shook.

"What are those?" I asked.

"Nothing," he said guiltily, then quickly pulled his coat

188 ◄ *Rich J. Stone*

sleeve over them.

"None of my business," I said. "Forget I mentioned it."

I watched them board the train and waved goodbye. Elizabeth looked happy. But Dodge looked pale as a ghost. Now that there was no turning back, I wondered if Dodge, the confirmed loner, was having second thoughts.

33.
Dodge: Second Thoughts, or
Cat Scratch Fever

I WAS HAVING TROUBLE BREATHING. The itsy-bitsy athlete was back in full swing—vaulting off my kidneys and using my bladder to break its fall. But I calmly took my seat next to Elizabeth on the train. His cat. Monty's fucking cat.

"Are you okay, Phil?" Elizabeth asked sweetly.

"Not sure," I managed to answer. "A little too much fresh air, maybe."

Elizabeth smiled and patted my hand. "As soon as we get you back to your filthy, polluted, crime-ridden city, you'll feel much better."

I forced a smile and held her hand, while absentmindedly stroking her bandages.

"Did you pack your gloves?" I asked, pointing to her suitcase.

"No. Briggs will have all that sent on ahead. I only packed the essentials for the time being."

"And gloves aren't essential, eh?" I asked.

"In the summer?"

"Well, you were wearing them quite a bit the last few days. I guess I just assumed . . ."

I trailed off waiting for a response.

"Do my gloves turn you on, Phil? Is that why you're so

interested in them?"

"As a matter of fact, they do. Very much so." I thought back to our all-too-brief encounter, when it was the only thing she wore. I also thought back to the first time I met Elizabeth—when I cradled her arm and pressed her soft hand to my lips. She was wearing a sleeveless dress with no gloves, then.

"Well, I'm sure I can pick up a pair in New York," she said. "I hear they have a store or two there." She laughed and kissed me.

I felt her hot lips on my mine. But I thought about Valerine Rizzo. If I had taken care of Valerine the way I was taking care of Elizabeth right now, I may very well have saved her life. Clearly, I was overcompensating with Elizabeth. For one thing, her life wasn't in any danger. I realized that now. And it was Maybach's fucking cat that provided the horrible clarity for me.

"Just suppose," I said, "that we were wrong. After all, Blake still hasn't confessed to the murder, and Lloyd will never confess to anything. The only thing we know for sure is that Chip, Blake and Eliot pulled a fast one on Bryce."

"What are you getting at?"

"Let's look at the facts. You received a letter. Bryce called me in to protect you. Someone driving Lydia's car fired a shot through your window using Lydia's gun." I paused. "You with me so far?"

"Yes," she answered.

"Continuing. Letter number two arrives to Bryce stating that Gaston had been kidnapped. Bryce is found dead the next day, accompanied by Gaston and letter number three. These are the facts and they are undisputed."

I stopped talking and looked out the window. It was a lovely evening in New England. The sun was just beginning to set over the picturesque landscape, rife with lush green rolling hills. It was a perfect backdrop to embark on a new life with Elizabeth. Why couldn't I just leave well enough alone?

"And?" she asked in anticipation. "Are you going to continue? The events didn't end there, surely."

"No," I said, "but the letters stopped there."

"Well, of course they did. Lloyd was the letter writer. And after Blake killed him, he was no longer able to write letters."

I switched my focus from the beautiful sunset to the scratch marks on my arm. Apparently, I was incapable of leaving well enough alone. "I don't think Lloyd wrote those letters," I said. "And I don't believe he took a shot at you, either."

"Then who did?"

"Bryce Danforth."

"You can't be serious."

"Why not? I found it rather curious that he hired me solely to be your bodyguard, and not to try and find the identity of the letter writer."

"That's because he knew it was Lloyd, and wanted to protect me."

"Did Bryce tell you that?"

"No. He didn't tell me anything. I knew nothing about the blackmail until you told me about it."

"Maybe that's because Bryce didn't want to protect you. Maybe he wanted you dead."

"I find that hard to believe, but I'm willing to hear you out. Go on, darling."

I needed to think first. What I was saying was just starting to come together at that very moment.

"Bryce writes a letter threatening you, borrows his wife's car and gun and takes a shot at you. Then, for argument's sake, let's say he writes a letter to himself about his own cat being kidnapped to throw me off the trail."

"But how could he have written the last letter? It was left at his own murder scene."

"Yes. And he was planning on committing a murder that night and leaving the note there. But he got bumped off before he could. Bryce's killer saw the note and decided to leave it at the scene to throw everyone off the trail."

"And who was Bryce planning on murdering?"

A fair question.

"Well, he had asked Maybach to meet him there early that morning," I said, thinking out loud. "Monty may have been an intended victim."

"But why would Bryce want to do such a thing?"

"He had a grudge against you. After you turned him down at the motel his ego couldn't handle it. And he also had good cause to have a grudge against your husband. He had Bryce's mother killed. Maybe Bryce found out about it when he took over as director. So he wanted to bring disgrace upon you both, and the cat show was the perfect venue for it. And Monty was getting a little too nosy."

Elizabeth thought for a moment. "You know, now that I hear you say it, it all seems so very plausible, Phil. Now, what about Wanda?" She squeezed my hand, excited to take part in the investigative process.

"Well, let's continue with the facts, shall we? Wanda is shot with a bullet from Lydia's gun, which is recovered at the scene, and then you end up going to the hospital with a case of mushroom poisoning."

"Yes?"

"Who could have had access to Lydia's gun?" I asked.

"Lydia?"

"Only if she killed Bryce," I answered.

"I'm not following you."

"We're still going under the assumption that Bryce was going to shoot Monty, and he was going to use Lydia's gun."

"Perhaps he was planning on framing Lydia for it," she offered.

"Maybe," I said. "And then whoever surprised Bryce with the sculpture, pried the gun out of Bryce's dead hand and then decided to continue with the frame job by taking another shot at your window, and dropping the gun on the ground for the cops to find. But this time, Wanda got in the way."

"And that inadvertently saved my life. Wanda very likely would have succeeded in poisoning me," Elizabeth said.

With a sudden lack of self-control, I pulled Elizabeth toward me and kissed her.

"It's okay, Phil," she whispered. "Wanda can't hurt me anymore."

I held her tight. I wanted to hold her forever. But then I thought about Valerine again. I put my own feelings ahead of the case with her as well. And I couldn't make the same mistake again. I released her from my embrace.

"I can't bring you back to New York with me," I said.

"Why?"

"This case hasn't been solved. It may still be too dangerous."

"How? No one's going to follow us to New York. We can put it all behind us."

"I was shot, Elizabeth. Right in the arm. Six inches to the left and it would've been through my heart. You think I can put that behind me?"

"Blake shot at you. That's obvious, isn't it? You were getting too close to discovering his gambling scheme."

I didn't say anything. Even though I knew for a fact that Rudolf was the gunman in that instance. I let Elizabeth continue.

"And Blake is going to prison for a very long time," she said, comforting me as if I were a child who had just had a bad dream. "He killed Lloyd. He obviously killed Bryce and Wanda, too."

"Whoever killed Bryce, killed Wanda. That's for certain. The big question is who catnapped Gaston?"

"That was either Eliot or Chip, right?" She pulled my head against her bosom, reassuring me that there were no more monsters under my bed. "It's all over, darling. We're going to have a fresh start together. And no one from Olde Sayville will be able to hurt either of us. I promise."

I held Elizabeth's hand. I stroked her bandages. It was time for me to speak my mind.

"But neither Eliot nor Chip had any of the tell-tale signs of a catnapper," I said. "A cat like Gaston probably would've put up a fight." I rolled up my sleeve and showed off my wound. "I got this from Monty's cat just for looking at it funny. I'd expect Gaston's captor to have something far worse."

"Well, then perhaps it was Bryce who faked the kidnapping. Just like you said. He must have written the letters, then."

"You backed off the Blake/Eliot/Chip theory pretty fast, didn't you?"

"Just trying to keep an open mind, darling."

"Why would Bryce kidnap his own cat?" I lashed out. "He was trying to frighten you. Did Gaston's kidnapping frighten you in any way?"

"No," she answered turning away and pouting. "But, as you've already postulated, perhaps he was attempting to misdirect you. Apparently it worked."

I resisted the urge to apologize for shouting at her. Each time she'd pulled that pouting act in the past, I immediately backed off. But not this time.

"You know what I did notice, though?" I said. "You. I noticed how incredibly beautiful you were—especially in those elbow-length gloves. And I fantasized about you and your elbow-length gloves. In fact, when we went to bed, that was the only thing you wore."

"Yes," she said with a mischievous smile. "I remember it well."

"But I realize now, that the timing of our encounter was a little suspect," I said staring out the window, unable to look her in the eye. "You suddenly couldn't control yourself when I suggested we go to the hospital. Maybe it was because you were afraid all the tests for poison would come up negative—and your scratch marks would be exposed." I turned and stared into her beautiful face. "You were the one that took Gaston."

The fog in my clouded mind was lifting. Before I stole Monty's Mercedes, Elizabeth was wearing a sleeveless dress with no gloves. It was Elizabeth who drove Monty to the club, because it was Briggs's day off. She'd have seen that Lydia was playing tennis with Lloyd, while Monty and I were engaging Bryce, thus giving her the opportunity to go in and grab Gaston. And since that incident, each time I saw Elizabeth, she was wearing either elbow-length gloves or long sleeves, even though it was unseasonably warm. She was covering up the scratches she got while taking Gaston.

"Phil, you don't know what you're saying."

But I did. And it got worse. Much worse.

"Don't I?" I shot back. "You never took that sleeping pill, either. It didn't make sense that it just wouldn't work. You waited for Maybach and me to leave, then you slipped out of the house and waited for Wanda to appear in the sitting room. You fired through the window and dropped the gun where you knew the police would be able to find it."

"How on earth could I have gotten my hands on Lydia's gun?" she said angrily.

"Maybe you took it when you stole Gaston," I said, even though I knew that wasn't how she had gotten the gun. I'd be getting to that part later; I needed to work out this portion of the crime first. "You killed Wanda in cold blood, just so you could frame Lydia," I drove the point home. "But when I started asking you questions about Wanda's death, you got scared and led me right to the poison as a misdirection. And I fell for it, baby. I believed that Wanda had been poisoning you, and that she poisoned the Judge as well. But now I know that it was you. You killed Wanda. And you killed your husband, too."

"Preposterous!" she snapped. "Why on earth would I do such a thing?"

"Because you were being blackmailed. Those photos of you and Bryce were taken before your husband's death. Not after. And Lloyd was blackmailing *you*, not Bryce. You knew if the Judge found out, he'd cut you out of his will and send you packing. You'd lose all that money. But if he was dead, you'd have nothing to worry about. So you poisoned him. That's when Lloyd saw he was no match for you, and figured he'd try to blackmail Bryce instead."

"You're making all of this up. Is this because you don't want me to come with you? You're just afraid of commitment."

"That may also be true, Elizabeth. But I fell in love with you, and you knew it. You used it to your advantage."

I thought back to our time together. Whenever I would start getting close to the truth was when she would become amorous. She took me to bed to avoid going to the hospital, which would have revealed her scratch marks, as well as showing absolutely no poison in her system. Then she all-of-a-sudden ordered me to leave the house and Olde Sayville altogether. When Maybach informed her that I had returned and was waiting in the car, she ingested a small portion of the poison, and scratched up her own arms to cover her tracks. Then she asked for the cat show to be cancelled, which would get Monty to leave town before he could uncover anything else. She was in the clear—until I was shot, that is. The shooting meant that neither Monty nor I would be leaving Olde Sayville as expected; so she met with me, told me she loved me, and planted the concept of Blake being dangerous in my head. And when she figured I had found the negatives, she conveniently confessed to some cockamamie "innocent" affair with Bryce.

"Too many things don't make sense," Elizabeth said defensively, interrupting my thought process. "What about Lloyd? Surely you don't think I killed him, do you?"

"No, I don't."

"So your entire fantastical tale doesn't hold water. Whoever killed Lloyd must have killed the others. And since the body happened to have been found in Blake's garage . . ."

"I don't recall telling you that the body was found in his garage. I believe my exact words were 'on Blake's premises.'"

"I assumed. I mean, he's not going to store a corpse in his dining room, is he?"

"No, he's not. But the simple fact of the matter is that Bryce killed Lloyd. I'm sure that after the police run their ballistics they'll find that the shot was fired from Lydia's gun. Bryce had arranged to purchase the negatives from Lloyd; then he double-crossed him and shot him. He was waiting for you to arrive with Gaston. You knew that Bryce had written the letter. You knew that Bryce had taken that shot at you. And that's why you catnapped Gaston. So you made a three-way deal—Bryce gets Gaston, Lloyd gets his money, and you get the negatives. But you wouldn't make the same mistake that Lloyd did—you figured Bryce would try to double-cross you and try to kill you that night. Bryce's plan was to make it look like Lloyd killed you and that he killed Lloyd in self-defense. Monty would arrive after the events occurred, just in time to back up Bryce's story. And he'd have the negatives there as supporting evidence. It didn't really matter to Bryce if the negatives were exposed, since Lydia already knew about it. But you were too smart for him. You knew you couldn't risk taking the car out in the middle of the night; not with a detective staying in your house. So you arranged for Lloyd to drive you over there, so as not to arouse suspicion. Then you found out that Lloyd was scheduled to meet Bryce much earlier than you were—that's when you figured it all out—but you decided to leave Lloyd in the dark about it. So you made sure that you and Lloyd arrived before Bryce did—you hid yourself away and calmly watched as he put a bullet through Lloyd. Then, you waited for the right moment, when Bryce had his back to you. It presented itself when he sat down in the wheelchair. That's when you snuck up behind him and crushed his skull with the heaviest thing you could find."

An affair gone wrong. A jealous and/or jilted lover. The numbers, dammit. The numbers never lie.

"But you couldn't leave Lloyd's body lying around there," I continued. "Too many questions for the police. So you dumped Bryce's body out of the wheelchair, and moved Lloyd's corpse into it. You wheeled Lloyd out to his car and put his body in the trunk. Then you dumped the wheelchair back in the office. This took a bit of time to accomplish, and when you returned, rigor mortis had already set in on Bryce. So you had to break his fingers to pry the gun out of Bryce's dead hand. You used that gun to shoot Wanda and frame Lydia. And this afternoon, while the entire town was busy at the banquet, you drove Lloyd's car into Blake's garage. Then you left an anonymous tip for the Chief suggesting that he search Blake's house. I wondered what the Chief had meant when he thanked me for the tip. After that you had nothing left to do but pack your bag and meet me at the station."

If Elizabeth was at all rattled by my accusation, she didn't let on. She was still composed and thinking clearly. "Assuming all this conjecture of yours is true," she said, "how can you prove it?"

"I can't," I said.

"Seems silly to even bring it up, then. Don't you agree?" she asked, with a bit of venom.

"You're absolutely right," I answered. "Because now I've got something on you, sweetheart—and you know it. When people have something on Elizabeth Hathorne, they don't tend to stay alive very long. All I can do now is make sure that I don't get bumped off because I know too much. So I guess the only way to protect myself is to make a pre-emptive strike."

Elizabeth gasped. I finally rattled her.

"Lots of people go missing in New York City every year," I said nonchalantly. "Hundreds of unsolved murders. Don't worry your pretty little head about it, though. I promise, when your time comes, you won't feel a thing."

Elizabeth looked at me. Her frightened expression became one of lust. She kissed me with all she had, and I let her. I got lost in her smell, in her taste. I flipped an imaginary coin in my head as I grabbed her and pulled her tight against me. But before the imaginary coin hit the imaginary ground, I felt the barrel of a very real gun sticking into my ribs.

"Tough guy, huh?" Elizabeth whispered in my ear. "But just stupid enough to fall for the same stunt again and again. Good thing for me your libido is so predictable."

"You'll never get away with it," I declared, not knowing what else to say.

"Sure I will. Like you said, there are hundreds of unsolved murders in New York City."

"Tell me something," I said. "What was the deal with you and Bryce, anyway?"

"It was complicated. He knew about my husband's corruption. The deal was that he'd keep it hushed up as long as I slept with him on a regular basis—and if I convinced the Judge to make Bryce next in line for the directorship. After my husband died, there was no need for me to continue sleeping with Bryce. I had as much dirt on him as he did on me. I suppose, deep in our hearts, we both knew it would come to this. One of us would end up killing the other. And when he made the first move with that ridiculous letter, that's when I knew I needed to kill him before he killed me. Which seems like a nice little segue for us, don't you think?"

"I was only bluffing. Wanted to see what you'd do. And I ended up getting a confession out of you."

"What an achievement," she said sarcastically.

"So you wrote the last two letters?"

"Of course," she said. "And I used the same printer that Bryce used for the first letter—the one in the director's office at the Society. But you never even got around to checking that, did you?"

The train began to slow down. We were getting ready to pull into the South Sayville Heights station.

"Change of plan. This is our stop now," she said. "Why don't you be a dear and carry my suitcase for me, Phil?"

I carried the suitcase down the aisle toward the exit. Elizabeth followed behind, her gun hidden away in her sleeve, but aimed right between my shoulder blades. I noticed a woman reading *The Great Gatsby* as I made my way down the aisle. It was the same woman that I'd met on the train a few days earlier.

"Not done with that thing yet?" I asked, startling her. She smiled at me and batted her eyes.

"I guess the planets are in alignment," she said.

"Sorry, love," I answered her. "Got the old ball and chain behind me."

"Not for much longer," Elizabeth muttered.

I couldn't get off the train with her. That would be the end. My only chance was to surprise her right then and there. And at that particular moment, I didn't much care whether I lived or died. All I cared about was that she got what was coming to her. If she shot me in front of all those witnesses, she'd never get away with it. I swung the suitcase backward, and hit Elizabeth squarely in her right elbow. I whirled around, and tried to slap the gun out her hand, but it was too late. She fired, and I felt a burning sensation in my chest. My knees buckled. During my descent, I saw several passengers leap up from their seats and wrestle Elizabeth to the ground. As I plummeted downward, the burning sensation moved across my chest and into my shoulder. Finally, I collapsed onto the lap of the woman whom I was destined to meet again.

"Everyone remain where you are," I heard the conductor shout. "The police are on their way."

I didn't fear death at that moment. I just thought about

Valerine Rizzo. Perhaps I'd be seeing her again; at least that way I could apologize to her. I touched my chest and brought my wet fingers to my face, so I could witness the last of my blood exiting my body. But it smelled like Scotch. The bullet had punctured the flask, which diverted the bullet's intended path to my heart and re-routed it to my shoulder. Pieces of glass and jagged metal from the flask had cut my chest open. But the wounds were only superficial. I thought back to all the doctors who told me that I needed to give up alcohol because it would kill me one day. The tiny gymnast in my stomach had taken a break from using my liver as a pommel horse, and sat quietly, sipping the Scotch. I looked up at the woman whose lap I had fallen upon.

"Have they accused Gatsby of making his fortune as a bootlegger, yet?" I asked.

"Several times," she answered softly. She gently stroked my forehead.

"Do you think it's true?" I asked.

"I don't think it matters."

"But what if–"

"Save it for the book club," she said, shushing me. I grasped her hand.

"My name's Phil," I said, introducing myself.

"Pleased to make your acquaintance," she answered dryly. "My name's Valerine."

Epilog.
Maybach: Odds and Ends

DODGE WAS TAKEN BACK TO OLDE SAYVILLE to recuperate from his gunshot wound and to formally press charges against Elizabeth. A few corridors down from Dodge's hospital room, the Colonel managed to get his hands on some narcotics and overdosed. In the Olde Sayville tradition of falsifying medical records, his death certificate said he died of natural causes. It closed the final chapter on the town's dark past—Johnny Maurier's man-made curse had claimed its ninth and final life.

With both leading contenders for the directorship of the Olde Sayville Society discredited and publicly shamed, and the Society's very existence exposed as a scam, the membership voted to disband it. The dry ordinance was officially overturned on June 14, 1996, and, shortly thereafter, the clubhouse was converted into an exclusive, members-only nightclub with several fully stocked wet bars.

Blake and Lydia were both cleared of murder charges, and Elizabeth was tried for the attempted murder of Dodge—apparently it was the only charge with enough evidence behind it that would hold up in court. Ms. Valerine Dotson also came to town to give her eyewitness testimony. She visited Dodge in the hospital and later accompanied him back to New York.

And as for me, when I returned home, I related this wonderful tale to my dear friend, Geoffrey, and proudly proclaimed that Dash and Lil, the Maybach cats, had solved yet another case.

ABOUT THE AUTHOR

RICH J. STONE is a native New Yorker, playwright, monologist and fiction writer. He holds a degree in chemistry from the University of Pennsylvania, but has yet to figure out what to do with it. *The Curse Had Nine Lives* is his second novel. His first novel, *Death Imitating Art*, is available at Amazon.com.

Visit his website at www.richjstone.com.